KT-394-378

TOMORROW, THE RIVER

GALWAY COUNTY LIBRARIES

BY DIANNE E. GRAY

HOUGHTON MIFFLIN COMPANY

BOSTON 2006

Copyright © 2006 by Dianne E. Gray
Interior illustrations © 2006 by Stephanie Cooper

All rights reserved. For information about permission to reproduce
selections from this book, write to Permissions, Houghton Mifflin Company,
215 Park Avenue South, New York, New York 10003.

www.houghtonmifflinbooks.com

The text of this book is set in Centaur.
"Point of Departure," a poem by Kirsten Dierking, to be published in her book *Northern Oracle*
(2007), was used with permission of Spout Press, Minneapolis, Minnesota.
Map on page xiii, by Leanne D. Knott, was used with permission of the cartographer.
Sources: ESRI Data, 2003. Projection: NIAD 83 UTM Zone 15.

Library of Congress Cataloging-in-Publication Data
Gray, Dianne E.
Tomorrow, the river / by Dianne E. Gray ; [illustrations ... by Stephanie Cooper].
p. cm.
Summary: In 1896, fourteen-year-old Megan joins her sister and family
on their steamboat for the summer
riding up the Mississippi River towards St. Paul, Minnesota,
and through all of their adventures, Megan realizes what is her "true calling."

ISBN-13: 978-0-618-56329-6 (hardcover)
ISBN-10: 0-618-56329-6 (hardcover)

[1. Sisters—Fiction. 2. Steamboats—Fiction.
3. Mississippi River—History—19th century—Fiction.
4. Photography—Fiction.]
I. Cooper, Stephanie (Stephanie Michelle), 1982– ill. II. Title.
PZ7.G7763Tom 2006
[Fic]—dc22
2005038068

Manufactured in the United States of America
VB 10 9 8 7 6 5 4 3 2 1

For my mother, Evelyn Folts

Acknowledgments

My heartfelt thanks to Kirsten Dierking for graciously allowing the use of her poem as this book's epigraph; Sue Montgomery and Kay Korsgaard, careful first readers; my daughter Leanne Knott, map-maker extraordinaire; my daughter Shelley Paulson, whose photographic eye provided inspiration; Mary Rockcastle and the College of Graduate Liberal Studies at Hamline University, for enduring lessons in craft; editor Kate O'Sullivan, for her vision; and Lee Gray—husband, best friend, saint.

TOMORROW, THE RIVER

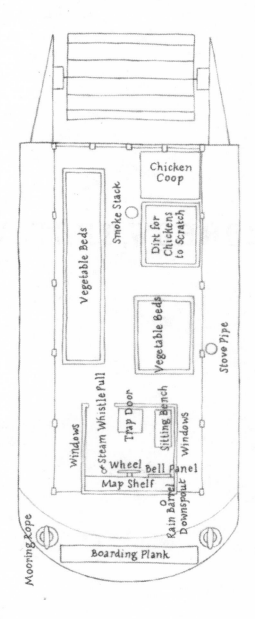

THE *OH MY*'S MAIN LEVEL FLOOR PLAN

Main Level

Bamboo Poles - lashed to underside of deck roof

Mooring Rope

Window

Window

Window

Bench

Bunks

Ladder

Table

Shelves

Flour
Sugar

Salted
Pork

Wood Box

Stove

Dry Sink

Larger Bed

Rain Barrel

Window

Window

Stove Pipe

Boarding Plank

Wheelbarrow

Window

Covered Wood Bin
(converts to cot)

Boiler

Engine

Workbench Saw
& Tool Storage

Window

Bicycle

A gull circles
and splashes down
and paddles into
a perfect circle
of sudden sun,
gray wings
lighted into
a radiant silver,
body a white
splendor of feathers,
the rise and fall
of waves against
the heart of the bird
as graceful as clouds.

It makes me think,
maybe a place
is waiting for us
where we leave behind
our clumsy feet,
our everyday clothing,
and swim for the spotlight,
our own shining time
on the water.

—Kirsten Dierking, Northern Oracle

Chapter 1

THE BURLINGTON AND MISSOURI EASTBOUND

June 26, 1896

I WASN'T MYSELF WHEN I BOARDED THE EASTBOUND. WEARING MY sisters' clothing didn't help. Hester's shoes were too big, and Lila's wedding suit was too long. The shoe caught the hem of the skirt, jerking me to a stop before I'd reached the top of the coach car steps. I might have freed myself if not for the handle of Mama's musty-smelling cartpetbag clutched in one hand and the lunch basket clutched in the other. As it was, I couldn't go forward, couldn't go back. I might still be in that predicament if the conductor hadn't tugged the skirt out from under the shoe and then raised the hem nearly to my knees so I could finish my climb without tripping up again. From the platform behind me, Mama gasped.

The conductor then took my elbow and guided me into the baggage section of the railway car. "Most passengers find that they have a more pleasant trip if they store their bags in the bins, miss," he said, reaching for Mama's carpetbag.

He didn't know my mama. She'd given me strict orders not to let go of the carpetbag *no matter what.* I shook my head and tightened my grip.

The conductor tightened his jaw.

The elbow again, and soon I was standing in the aisle of the coach car's seating section, running through the list of where I should and should not sit. "Sit with a woman. Not a painted-up woman, but a fresh-scrubbed one. A grandmotherly type would be good," Mama had said. "And don't sit with a man, especially not a smooth-talking, slick-dressing dandy," my sister Hester had advised. "Above all, don't sit in a seat by yourself. It'd be like saying, 'Come on over' to all those smooth-talking, slick-dressing dandies," my sister Lila had added with a finger wag. Then there was my brother Joey's advice: "Sit up front with the engineer and save yourself all the trouble." Joey was twelve.

What Mama and my sisters hadn't figured on was a car with only five other passengers, all of whom were men. The conductor, again, saying that the train would be pulling out soon and why didn't I take the first empty seat on my right. I did as I was told, fitted the carpetbag onto my lap and the lunch basket close beside me, and then turned to wave at Mama through the window. Mama might have waved back if she hadn't been straining to free herself

TOMORROW, THE RIVER

from the lock Hester and Lila had on her. And she might have smiled if her lips hadn't been talking so fast. I couldn't make out her exact words, but I guessed she was letting her worry out.

Mama thought fourteen was too young for a girl to travel alone. But Mama had her rules. She couldn't very well have said no to my spending the summer as a mother's helper to my sister Hannah, when she'd already promised me to Lila when Lila's new baby arrived in September and to Hester when Hester's new baby arrived in November. Mama's rules would have lost their wings, though, if she'd have known about the letter I'd secretly sent to Hannah, begging her to invite me and promising to pay my own way.

Being a mother's helper wasn't new to me. Since passing the eighth-grade exam at Harmony School a year ahead of all the other girls my age, Mama had hired me out to two of my cousins' families, all with new babies in the house, though the help that was required had nothing to do with cooing or cuddling. I'd cooked and scrubbed, tended to the older children, mended and ironed. My wages had been half of what I might have earned if working for a family I wasn't related to. The important thing, as Mama had reminded me repeatedly, was "invaluable practice." But practice wasn't something I could hold in the palm of my hand and count.

As it was, I'd earned only enough money to purchase the $11.50 railway ticket that had gotten me aboard the Eastbound, and a $3.50 return ticket that would get me only partway home. Mama didn't know about the partway-home part. I'd have to figure out a way to earn myself all the way home, and I had a start. Mama had given me two dollars from her egg money. "For telegrams," she'd said, pinning the bills to the inside of my camisole. *How much could a few words cost?*

Hester and Lila were still holding Mama back when the train began to pull away. When *I* began to pull away. I grabbed onto Mama then, too, holding her with my eyes. Holding and holding . . . a lump forming in my throat and expanding with each of the steam locomotive's chug-a-choos. Holding and holding . . . until my eyes got to stinging so bad I couldn't help but rest them with a long blink. When my eyes opened again it was as if someone had flipped the page in a picture book. Prairie Hill station had been replaced by the corral behind Wilson's livery stable, and Mama had been replaced by a swayback horse. Another blink and the horse turned into a mangy old dog pawing through a pile of rubbish behind Sloan's Eatery, and then the dog blurred into a gravedigger throwing dirt in the Methodist church cemetery.

By the time the backside of Prairie Hill had given way to cornfields, the chug-a-choos were packed so tightly together I couldn't tell where one ended and the next began—*ch-ch-ch-ch.* A snake-spooked horse gallops pretty fast, especially when you're riding bareback and holding on for dear life, but even the healthiest horse would have dropped dead in its tracks after a quarter mile of trying to race the Eastbound. The telegraph poles sailed past my window as if tick marks on a measuring stick—counting me farther away from home, farther away from Mama and her worried-sick heart. When the locomotive approached the first road crossing, I swear I heard real words mixed in with the steam whistle's mournful cry— *poooooor Mama.* There was no holding back my tears after that.

I fumbled in the carpetbag for my handkerchief, all the while sniffling and thinking about how lost Mama was going to be without me. Of her four daughters, I was the only one still living at home. Hester and Lila lived nearby and visited often, though Mama said that wasn't the same. There was one other woman in the house—my brother Jake's wife, Alice. But Mama and Alice didn't see eye to eye on much of anything. Mama dredged her chicken pieces in flour; Alice dredged in cornmeal. Mama believed open windows were good for our health; Alice believed open windows let in too much dust and barnyard stink. *With me away, who will take Mama's side?* I dug deeper in the carpetbag and came up with, instead of my handkerchief, a splendid, tear-drying idea. I'd get off the Eastbound at the next stop and wait for the Westbound to whisk me back to Prairie Hill. I'd do it for Mama!

When the Eastbound steamed away from Highland station, I was still onboard. I hadn't abandoned my plan to return home for

GALWAY COUNTY LIBRARIES

Mama, only postponed it. I'd need a good story for why I'd cut my journey short, and I'd been too busy gawking out the window to come up with one. The freshly sprouted fields and cow-dotted pastures were no different from those on our farm, except that I was seeing them from a fast-moving perch. The rows of corn, which farmers took pride in planting arrow-straight, appeared to angle toward one another until coming together at a far-distant and perplexing point. Thinking I might be able to set the rows straight again, I crossed my eyes. This caused an even more startling sight. It was as if the train was standing still and the world outside the window was racing past, instead of the other way around. Then I remembered one of Mama's scoldings, "Cross your eyes and they'll stay that way." I uncrossed, and the outside world dug in its heels and skidded to a stop.

Halfway between the Highland and Denton stations, the sky darkened and rain spattered the coach car windows. I occupied myself watching the raindrops perform a watery version of the Virginia reel. Two droplets reached out to one another as if in a curtsy and bow, then the two became one and cut a downward path through the other droplets. Two, then four, then six, and then eight, pairing and sliding into a shimmering rivulet. I could have watched the droplets dance for hours, if my hot breath hadn't fogged up the window.

I turned my attention to the interior of the coach car. The car was shaped like a loaf of bread—flat sides with a curved top. The walls were lined with polished wood the color of dark rye. The plush-looking seats weren't out-of-the-oven doughy soft, but they weren't hard either. They sat more like day-old. All those thoughts of bread led to thoughts of hunger. My hunger. Before taking a bite out of the thick hunk of wheat bread Mama had packed for me, I raised it to my nose. It smelled of home. Though Mama had intended the bread to last the whole of the twenty-four-hour train trip, I was suddenly ravenous and gobbled the entire hunk in that one sitting, which left only the jerked beef, dried apricots, and crumbled applesauce cookies to fold back into the paper and return to the belly of my lunch basket.

I didn't get off at the Denton station, because the rain had turned into a gully washer. Mama's Sunday hat, Hester's spare pair of shoes, and Lila's worsted wedding suit were loans, not hand-me-downs I could keep. I had strict orders that these things be returned—uncrushed, unscuffed, unstained, untorn, un-rained-on, un-anything.

The rain had let up by the time the Eastbound stopped at the castle-like station in Lincoln, the first real city—its backside, anyway—I'd ever seen, but I didn't get off there either. Didn't dare. Not after turning down smooth, slick man's offer.

I'd been bent over the carpetbag, double-checking to see if my partway-home railway ticket was still tucked inside my everyday left shoe, when a silky-sounding male voice asked, "First time away from home?"

I glanced up. The man's hair was slicked back with pomade, and the suit of clothes he wore looked like it had come from the most expensive pages in the *Sears, Roebuck Catalogue.* "Oh no, sir, I'm in the army . . . no, I mean my *husband* is in the army, and I'm on my way to join him. He's burly." This was a story Lila had cooked up. Like a cake made with too few eggs, it flopped. Smooth, slick man slid into my seat. His smile smelled of cigars, which wasn't surprising since he soon told me he was a cigar salesman from Chicago. By the time the train pulled into Lincoln station, his destination, I knew everything there was to know about the cigar business, and smooth, slick man had invited me to get off the train with him so he could teach me how to smoke one. "All the finest women in Chicago are smoking cigars these days," he'd said, winking.

The train was scheduled to stay at Lincoln station for thirty minutes, to take on fresh supplies of water and coal, so there would have been time to take smooth, slick man up on his offer, but I turned him down. Not because I was squeamish about trying something new, and not because Mama had told me not to get off the train *No matter what.* I turned down his offer because of that wink. I'd learned the meaning behind winks without needing any lectures from Mama or my sisters. Every wink that had come my way had come from boys who wanted to steal a kiss behind the schoolhouse.

The coach car was nearly filled when the conductor called "All aboard!" at Lincoln station. I might have looked around for someone else to sit with, someone who looked like they hadn't winked in a good long while, if I hadn't been sitting in that one spot for so long that it had started to feel kind of homey. A couple of folks tarried at the edge of my seat, but all moved on up the aisle when they saw that the unoccupied half was taken up by Mama's carpetbag.

When the chug-a-choos started up again, my face was buried in the *Burlington and Missouri Traveler's Guide*. In three more hours, the train would be crossing the Missouri River at Plattsmouth. I thought on that for a while and decided it would be foolish of me to have come so far without at least letting my eyes soak in a real river before returning home.

Upon leaving Lincoln, the tracks nosed northeast. The land turned hilly, and the coach car swayed as the tracks curved this way and that through the valleys. Swayed so much at times that folks trying to walk in the aisle were forced to grab hold of seatbacks. That's how I came to make the acquaintance of Horace Blount. He'd been down the aisle before, asking those with newspapers if they'd pass the papers on to him when they'd finished reading them. He was making his way down the aisle a second time, his nose stuck in one of those hand-me-down newspapers, when a particularly tight curve landed him in my seat and his newspaper in my lap.

"Sorry, miss," he said, then pulled Mama's crushed carpetbag out from under him and set about tugging on the sides as if trying to restore its shape.

I set about refolding the newspaper while reading Horace with a sideways glance. He looked to be seventeen or eighteen. Beneath his patchy beard, his face was quite handsome. There was a button missing from his vest, his shirt lacked starch, his collar was frayed, and his shoes showed the scuffs of hard wear. Having assured myself that he failed the slick-dresser test, I boldly thrust my right hand in his direction. "I'm Megan Barnett. Nice to make your acquaintance."

"Horace Blount," he said, giving my hand a sturdy shake before returning his smiling eyes to Mama's carpetbag.

"I see you like newspapers," I said.

"Yes, miss, I read them from first page to last."

I waited, hoping he would continue. He didn't, so I asked another question, "What is your destination?"

"Plattsmouth, miss."

"Do you have business there?"

"Yes, miss."

No doubt remained. Horace definitely wasn't a smooth talker, though Mama and my sisters had also warned me to watch out for "the quiet ones." This was confusing because my papa wasn't much for words, and Mama had married him. When I'd asked Papa's permission to spend the summer with Hannah, all he'd said was, "Best ask your ma." And there was my brother, James. James was so quiet he made Papa look like a chatterbox. About all you got from James was a nod or a shoulder shrug. Mama and my sisters were worried that James's shyness would keep him from finding a nice girl to marry. In fact, Horace reminded me of James. Perhaps all the quiet ones needed was some practice, and Plattsmouth was still two hours away.

"What sort of business, if you don't mind my asking?"

"Doors, miss."

"Doors?"

Horace handed me the carpetbag, which he'd tugged nearly to its original shape. "Are you always this full of questions, if you don't mind my asking?"

"No, not usually. I . . . I need the practice."

"Practice?"

"You see, I'm on my way to meet up with my sister. My sister is married, and I barely know her husband, and I want to get off on my best foot with him, so I . . . thought I'd polish my getting-to-know-you conversation skills on you."

Horace grinned. "So I'm your experiment, then?"

"I . . . I . . . I'm sorry."

"No, don't be sorry. Experiments are right up my alley. I'm an engineering student at the University of Nebraska."

Mama and my sisters hadn't given a word of warning about college boys, probably because they'd never dreamed that I'd run into one.

"So you're engineering doors, then?" I asked.

"Working summers in my uncle's door factory hasn't a lick to do with engineering, I'm sorry to say. I work there to earn the money for my tuition. If I had been born into a wealthy family, like most of the fellows back at school, I wouldn't be on this train right now, wouldn't be spending my summer choking on sawdust. I'd be building my dream."

"Your dream?"

"Have you ever heard of horseless carriages?"

"Yes, I've heard tell of them, but my papa says that no machine will ever replace the horse and that anybody who believes otherwise is a fool."

Horace grinned so big he showed his gums. "Guess that makes me a fool then. It's my aim to be one of the fellows that build them."

Papa had left the warnings up to Mama and my sisters, but if he'd known ahead of time that I'd be sharing my seat with a fellow who was planning to put wheels on foolishness and drive it around, he'd have had more than a few words to say about it.

Horace put his hands behind his head and stretched out his legs like he was fixing to stay awhile. "A person would be a fool *not* to follow their dreams, if you ask me. How about you? What dream are you dreaming for yourself?"

My dream? Mama had said there were only two dreams a girl

could have—become a teacher and then marry a God-fearing man and have a houseful of babies, or skip the teaching part altogether and go right to the altar, like all of my sisters had done. I wasn't about to say words like *marriage* and *babies* for fear Horace would start thinking about how one led to the other and get the wrong idea, so I shrugged my shoulders.

"But everyone has a dream, some just haven't discovered it yet. Why don't you start by telling me what you're good at. Everybody's good at something."

All the good-ats in my family were taken. Hannah was good at make-believe. So good that she wrote plays, one of which would be performed by a theater group in St. Paul, Minnesota, that August. Hester was a wizard in the kitchen, and Lila could turn a piece of muslin into an embroidered work of art. James had a way with the farm animals, and Jake was good at sensing just the right day to begin planting or harvesting the crops. Jon and Jacob, who had stood on the two rungs just above mine in the stair steps of our family and had died in a blizzard, were good at being angels. And Joey was good at arithmetic and good at being charming.

There *was* one thing I was good at, though Mama had always said I should keep it to myself else people would think me not quite right in the head. I sure didn't want Horace to think of me that way, so I told him the only thing about me that I'd ever heard Mama boast about. "I'm good at being good."

"I've no doubt that you are. But there must be something else, something you can finagle into a dream."

I'd been wrong about Horace. He wasn't a quiet fellow; he was a whittler. Just like Mama. Whittled away and didn't stop until all that was left was the truth. Horace would be getting off the Eastbound at Plattsmouth and I'd never lay eyes on him again, so I figured I might as well get it over with and give him what he wanted. "Promise you won't laugh?"

"I promise."

I leaned close to his ear and whispered, "I'm good at seeing things."

"Tell me more."

I looked around for a good example. Pointing at the ornate lantern hanging from the ceiling, I asked, "What do you see?"

"I see a lantern," Horace answered.

"Yes, it's a lantern, but that's not what I see first. I see light that's trapped like a wild critter in a cage. And the light that does escape is softer, easier on the eye. Happier, somehow."

"Hmmm. What do you see there, in that overhead luggage rack?"

"I see a geometry problem—curves and angles and points of intersection. It's solid and fixed, but if you lean your head one way or the other, the angles and curves move and change shape. Some shorten; some lengthen. And see there, where the backside of that bar is blocked from the light? See how dull and colorless it is? No light—no color."

And that's how we passed the miles to Plattsmouth. Horace would point to an object and I'd tell him what I saw. He'd listen, then scrunch his brow and study the object for himself. Once he got the hang of it, Horace became quite good at seeing, too. A woman two rows ahead was wearing a hat with a peacock feather attached. To Horace, the feather was a quill pen and the hat was a flattened inkwell. To me, the entire peacock had nested under the hat and poked one of its feathers through the weave so the eye at its tip could see. I'd just finished telling Horace this when the hat woman turned her head and the shimmering feather eye looked to be staring straight at us, knowingly. I giggled into my hand and Horace slapped his knee.

Sitting next to Horace, chatting and seeing with him, was like wearing shoes that fit. Comfortable and cozy. And while we chatted and saw, I memorized Horace, stored him away in my mind's eye hoping never to forget. The small scar on his left cheek, the square bow of his jaw. The sheen of his black hair. His fresh-air scent. The melody in his voice. His sturdy, steady hands as he opened the folds in a piece of paper, revealing his design for the automobile he was hoping one day to build.

When we arrived at Plattsmouth station, Horace wasn't in a hurry to leave my seat. He'd check his pocket watch, then say, "Well, I suppose I should be going," stand, then sit back down and ask what I saw in one of the station's pushcarts or a lamppost or in the shadows of the conductor's oddly shaped ear. On his last standing-up, he said, "I'm such a clod. Here we've been sitting to-gether all this time and I haven't asked where exactly you're headed, and what you'll be doing once you get there."

"Burlington, Iowa, to spend the summer traveling up the Mississippi River on my brother-in-law's steamboat."

Horace's eyes bugged, and then he started saying, "The Mississippi River. The Mississippi River," over and over like the words were doing backward somersaults on his tongue.

It wasn't until the Eastbound had begun to move ahead that Horace finally said something else. "Megan Barnett, you are the most delightful young woman I've ever met." I should have said something back, something about him not being a fool after all, but my heart was fluttering so furiously I couldn't catch my breath.

Once outside, Horace, a canvas duffle slung over his shoulder, kept pace with my window. I didn't blink. Not even when Horace, who was looking at me instead of where he was going, sprinted right off the edge of the wooden platform. He scrambled to his feet and managed one last wave before he slipped from my sight. Leaving Horace behind was like leaving home for the second time in a day. No, worse. I'd be returning home at the end of summer, but I'd likely never lay eyes on Horace again.

I didn't let my eyes tear up, though they wanted to. Tears would have kept me from seeing Horace's door factory, which he'd said stood next to the railway tracks three blocks to the west of the

Missouri River Bridge. I missed it. Not because I blinked, but because it was impossible to see through the churning cloud of thick, black smoke.

When the coach car breathed blue air again, the land was falling away, and, if not for the crisscross of bridge trusses and the clatter of the wheels on the tracks, I might have thought I was flying. I gripped the edge of my seat and looked down. Water. Wide water. Moving water, on its way to someplace else. Someplace grand.

Soon enough, the land rose up again, and the Eastbound picked up speed, leaving Horace and his river behind. My river was still nineteen hours and the whole state of Iowa away. I settled back in my seat. *Tomorrow, the river,* I thought. *Tomorrow, I'll be someplace grand.*

MAN INJURED

KEOKUK, IOWA—Many were heard to exclaim, "Oh my!" when a riverboat steamed into Keokuk late Thursday. Onboard the small stern-wheeler, aptly named the *Oh My,* were Mr. Isaac Bradshaw, a resident of New Orleans, Louisiana, and his wife and young son. More "Oh mys!" rose up when it was learned that Mr. Bradshaw had met with misfortune earlier in the day. When trying to help the crew of another vessel free a logjam, he'd lost his footing and badly injured a leg. Keokuk's Doctor Smith was hastily summoned and, after a thorough examination of Mr. Bradshaw, recommended that the leg be amputated. Mr. Bradshaw insisted that treatment would have to wait, however, because the *Oh My* was on its way to Burlington to meet his wife's fourteen-year-old sister, Megan Barnett, at the railway station there. The *Oh My,* piloted by Bradshaw's wife, Hannah, steamed away from Keokuk just after dawn this morning. This reporter wishes Mr. Bradshaw and his family Godspeed.

Chapter 2

I O W A

AFTER MEETING HORACE, I ALL BUT FORGOT ABOUT MY PLAN TO RETURN home for Mama. Instead, I divided my thoughts between Horace and Hannah. Thinking of Horace was like swallowing a halo; thinking of Hannah was like swallowing a swarm of butterflies. Hannah had been my favorite sister when I was a little girl. If I fell and scraped my knee, Hannah would tell me that I'd fallen not because I was clumsy, like Mama always said, but because a trickster troll living under the ground had reached up and grabbed my ankle. Then, when I was seven, Hannah married Isaac Bradshaw and they'd gone off to live in New Orleans, Louisiana. Hannah's magic went with her, and I became "clumsy Megan" again.

Hannah had returned home but twice. Her first visit, in the summer of 1891, had been to introduce her son, Jon-Jacob, to the family. Hannah visited the second time in the fall of 1894 to help the family celebrate our move out of the old sod house and into the new two-story, wood-framed house Papa had built for Mama. "I needed to see the house with my own eyes to believe it," Hannah had said to Mama when Papa was out of earshot. Between visits, my memory of what Hannah looked like faded back to the way she looked before she'd gone away. So, when the grown-up Hannah, the wife and mother Hannah, stepped off the Westbound at Prairie Hill station, she'd seemed more stranger than sister.

And there I was, on my way to spend the summer with a sister I barely knew and a brother-in-law I knew even less. And Jon-Jacob. Jon-Jacob had taken a shine to me on their last visit. Other than his mama, I was the only one who could pick Jon-Jacob up without him making a fuss, which greatly vexed *my* mama. He'd sit on my lap and stare so hard into my eyes it was as if he was reading the most fascinating of books. I hoped Jon-Jacob hadn't forgotten me, as was too often the case back home. People would regularly ask, "Which Barnett girl are you?" or mistake me for one of my sisters. Even Mama. I'd be Lila, or Hester, though not once had she mistakenly called me Hannah. I was Megan, the forgettable.

Horace was not the last to share my seat, though none were as pleasant. There was the Reverend Herman, who was traveling from town to town and seat to seat, thumping his Bible and shouting that

July the thirty-first would be the day of Armageddon. "Judgment day is at hand. Are you prepared?" he asked when he slid into my seat. I stammered something about having been baptized, but that must not have been good enough for the Reverend. He laid a hand hard on the top of Mama's blue hat and prayed for my soul. After he finished his praying, he asked if I might have an offering for God's messenger, "A morsel of food perhaps?" He might have been the devil himself, but I wasn't taking any chances. I handed over what was left of my paper-wrapped lunch.

And Rufus Hanrahan, a traveling sheepshearer, smelled as if he had taken his last bath in a tub of eye-stinging sheep dip.

No, none was as pleasant as Horace.

DOOR FACTORY BURNS

PLATTSMOUTH, NEBRASKA— Despite the Plattsmouth Fire Department's best efforts, the Blount Door Factory burned to the ground earlier today. A spark from a recently installed system of electric lights is suspected as the cause. Several workers suffered burns, though all are expected to recover. Mr. William Blount, the factory owner, vows to rebuild, though he estimates that rebuilding could take several months. In the meantime, he regrets to say that his employees will have to find other work.

Chapter 3

A GRANDMOTHERLY TYPE

AFTERNOON HAD FADED INTO EVENING AND EVENING INTO PITCH-black night when I finally shared my seat with a person Mama would have approved of—Mrs. Gertrude Galt, a white-haired, grandmotherly type. Gertrude was good at names. In no time at all, she'd told me the names of her twelve children and forty-two grandchildren, their dates of birth, where each lived, which ones had made something of themselves, and which ones had turned out to be "no-accounts." Mrs. Galt had nearly as many ailments as she had children, and she spoke of them with equal zest. She'd had lumbago, shingles, dropsy, gout, gallstones and kidney stones, hives, and a variety of digestive complaints, and was on her way to visit a doctor in Des Moines who was said to cure all manner of ills with a machine that would send electrical shocks through her body.

What Gertrude forgot to add to her list of ailments was a bad case of sleep-itis. In the middle of naming which ladies in her church circle were good housekeepers and which were not, which nagged their husbands and which did not, her head fell to my shoulder and she was asleep. I began to yawn. I thought about using Gertrude's head as my pillow, though I wasn't sure which ailments she might still have or if they might be catching, so I leaned my head back against the seat, closed my eyes, and tried counting some of Rufus Hanrahan's sheared sheep. The sheep weren't cooperative. Without their wool coats, all they could do was stand there on the far side of the dream fence and shiver.

Eyes open again, I was startled to see that a thread of Gertrude's spittle was trailing into a puddle on the bodice of Lila's wedding suit. I didn't want to be disrespectful to an elder, but I didn't want to get one of her diseases either, so I nudged Gertrude awake, and she picked up right where she'd left off—naming church ladies. It went on like that—chatter, then sleep, chatter, then sleep—until the conductor called Gertrude's stop.

I must have caught the sleep-itis from Mrs. Galt. The last thing I remember is removing my nightshirt from Mama's carpetbag, wadding it into a ball, and tucking it between my head and the window. The next thing I remember after that was waking to find myself curled up on the seat, and daylight was screaming at my eyes. The conductor strolled down the aisle about then, and though I was afraid to ask, I knew I must. "Sir, may I ask where we are just now?"

He grinned. "Next stop, Burlington, Iowa."

INMATE ESCAPES

FORT MADISON, IOWA—Samuel Silver, a twenty-year-old vagrant held on the charge of assault and burglary, escaped from the Fort Madison Jail around seven o'clock last evening. Unwittingly assisting in Mr. Silver's escape was the jailer's seventeen-year-old daughter, Melinda Bates. Though her story has altered slightly with each telling, it appears that Mr. Silver charmed her into unlocking his cell door when she brought him his supper. Miss Bates was unharmed, though understandably shaken. Though it is thought that Mr. Silver has left town, the good citizens of Fort Madison are warned to be on guard. Mr. Silver is of medium build, and at the time of his escape was wearing gray trousers, white shirt, and a brown tweed vest. Miss Bates was overheard to describe him as "quite good looking."

Chapter 4

BURLINGTON STATION

I FELT LIKE A NEWBORN CALF WHEN I STEPPED OFF THE TRAIN AND ONTO the Burlington station platform. My legs were wobbly and my empty stomach was bawling for something, anything, to eat. My eyes were wide open, though, hopscotching from one face to another, trying to pick Hannah's face, grown-up or otherwise, out of the crowd.

The Eastbound huffed away, the platform emptied of people, and still I stood there; it was as if the soles of Hester's shoes were bolted to the bricks. The sudden quiet was deafening. The stillness, after all that moving, made me dizzy, and something besides hunger churned in my stomach. With all the "If this happens—do that" instructions Mama and my sisters had given me, they'd forgotten to include the most important. It hadn't seemed necessary, I suppose.

Hannah had promised to meet my train, and Hannah was good at keeping promises.

It occurred to me then that Hannah must be waiting for me inside the station. The station, which hadn't existed when I'd been concentrating on faces, loomed to fill the space in front of me. Built of red brick, the building's grand size shouted of its importance. Important places, like churches, had rules that were known only to those who belonged. I didn't see that I had a choice, so I got my weak knees moving and was soon inside. My footsteps echoed off the sky-high ceiling as I weaved between the pew-like benches, peering into strange faces. The door to the ladies' toilet chirped when I went inside and groaned when I came back out.

My heart pumping perspiration to my forehead, I chose an empty bench where I could keep an eye on both the front and back doors, then sat down and tried to gather my wits. *Hannah had been delayed, but she was on her way. Surely she was. Any minute, she'd come bursting through one of the doors. Yes, she'd burst through the door on the next tick of the station clock. The next tick, or the next.*

Ticks that sounded like scolding tongue tsks. *Tsk—you should have stayed home in Nebraska. Tsk—your mama was right, fourteen is too young to travel alone. Tsk—only you, Megan Barnett, clumsy Megan, forgettable Megan, good-only-at-being-good Megan, could get yourself into this kind of fix. Tick, tsk, tick, tsk.*

I tore my gaze away from the clock and focused on other

things. The grain of the wood in the front door, the interesting pattern of chalk dust on the floor beneath the board listing arrivals and departures, the spider building a web in the corner of a window. The young man sitting on a bench opposite mine, pretending to be asleep. I knew he wasn't actually sleeping because, every now and again, I'd catch him lifting an eyelid and looking about. As often as not, his eye was pointed in my direction. He was quite a handsome fellow and nicely dressed in gray trousers and a tweed vest, so I didn't know whether to be perturbed or pleased.

Much as I tried, my eyes kept returning to the station clock's minute hand and its incessant counting. Forty-four . . . fifty-six . . . one hundred and nine . . . tick, tick, tick. One hundred and fifty-six, and then a blur of movement in the corner of my eye. My head jerked to the side just as Hannah left by way of the front door.

"Here, I'm here!" I shouted, leaping up and running after her. "Wait!" I called as I stepped outside. "Hannah, stop, please stop," I pleaded as I tried to rub the sun-blind from my eyes. Hannah did stop, then turned and walked toward me. She laid a hand on my arm. "Are you in need of assistance, miss?" she asked.

The woman, who looked like Hannah to about the same degree that a dandelion looks like a daffodil, waited for my answer, then asked me again if I needed help. I mustered my most convincing voice and answered, "Oh, no. I'm fine. I . . . I mistakenly thought you were my sister."

The woman smiled, then turned and walked away. I stared after her. She seemed nice, motherly, in fact. Perhaps I'd been too hasty in turning down her offer of help. I cleared my throat and raised a hand. An empty hand!

To my small relief, Mama's carpetbag was still there on the station bench where I'd left it. To my horror, the carpetbag's contents were strewn hither and yon, and there was a hand inside—a hand belonging to the pretending-sleep fellow. I raced up to him, and when he saw me his arms shot into the air as if he were a soldier in surrender. "No harm meant, miss. I was only putting your things back into your bag." He then thrust out his right hand for a shake. "Name's Seth. Seth Martin."

I ignored his hand. "Why did you take my things out of the bag in the first place?"

"Wasn't me, miss. There was another fellow, a shady-looking fellow. He's the one that was digging in your bag. I think I scared him off before he could take anything, but you might want to check."

I snatched a pair of my bloomers from the floor and looked up. "Would you mind?"

Seth turned away.

I took stock. My underthings were accounted for, my two shirts, two skirts, nightshirt and cotton stockings, my hairbrush and my handkerchief, my apron and my everyday pair of shoes. My everyday shoes! I jammed a hand into first one and then the other.

I turned them upside down and shook them out; all the while a hole was opening in my heart. Finding only emptiness, I slumped onto the bench.

"What is it? Is something missing?" Seth asked.

It was hard to answer when all of Mama's warnings about not letting go of the carpetbag *no matter what* clogged my throat.

"Here, have a sip," Seth said, sliding a canteen off his shoulder and unscrewing the cap.

I gulped, noisily, then, with water dripping from my chin and the seed of a plan sprouting in my head, I stood and took a step in the direction of the ticket window. Seth caught my arm. "Are you okay?"

"My return railway ticket . . . it's missing. I need to explain what happened to the ticket agent and ask him for a new one."

Seth rolled his brown eyes. "Ticket agents have heard every hard-luck story in the book from people wanting a free ride."

"Surely he'll believe me."

"There's plenty of young women—pretty young women like yourself—who, for one reason or another, have taken up sinful ways. How's the ticket fellow to know which are telling the truth and which are serving up lies with their long eyelashes and smiles?"

"But I have to try."

"You'd best let me talk to him, then. Some say, if I set my mind to it, I can charm a buffalo into handing over his hide."

"You'd do that for me?"

"Anything for a damsel in distress," Seth said as he bowed in a gentlemanly way.

I watched Seth's back as he spoke with the man behind the ticket window. And after he talked for a bit, the agent looked up at me and smiled. Then Seth talked some more and the ticket agent smiled some more and then shuffled some papers and then Seth stuffed something into his hip pocket.

Seth turned and walked back to me, his smile fading a bit with each step. "Sorry, I tried my darnedest, but I couldn't convince him."

"But . . . he gave you something. I thought—"

"Oh, that. Just a lowly train schedule."

"Did you tell him about the thief?"

"Yep, but he claims he didn't see any thief."

"Did you tell him that you saw the thief?"

"I did, but I think he figures the two of us are in cahoots."

"The constable, then. I must go tell the local constable. Could you direct me?"

Seth's left eyebrow shot up. "And what would you tell *him?*"

"I'd tell him that a thief stole my ticket."

"And when he asked you why you've been loitering in the railway station, you'd answer . . ."

"My sister was supposed to meet my train, but she has been detained."

"And when he asked if you had any money, you'd answer . . ."

"Why would he want to know if I have any money?"

"Because constables don't like broke folks hanging out in their towns, figure they'll turn to thievery quick enough."

"Then I'd tell him I have two dollars."

"And do you?"

I nodded.

"Well then, the constable will ask why the thief didn't steal your money along with your railway ticket."

"I'd tell him the money wasn't in the carpetbag."

Seth's right brow then shot up to join his left. "I see. So you've got it hidden in your clothes someplace, have you?"

I might have blushed if not for a question that was burning to be asked. "How is it that you know so much about constables?"

"I had me a job in a jailhouse down in Chillicothe once, sweeping floors and the like. A fellow can learn a lot if he just keeps his eyes open."

"And how is it that you happen to be here in the station?"

"Guess you might say I'm in the same boat as you. I was on my way upriver, to St. Paul, for some work, and this is as far as I got before my money ran out."

"What now?" I asked.

"I'll think of something. I always do. How about you?"

"I don't see that I have a choice but to sit here until my sister arrives."

Seth stretched his legs out then and put his hands behind his head like Horace had done on the train. "Would you like a little company while you wait?"

I looked up at the station clock for the first time in twenty-three minutes. Seth wasn't Horace, but he was good at making time move more quickly. "I guess I don't mind," I said.

Seth wasn't much interested in talking about himself. Instead he was interested in me. He was especially interested when I told him about Hannah and Isaac's riverboat. "A gambling boat?" he asked, perking up like a collar that had just been starched.

"No. Hannah would never—" A loud stomach growl interrupted my sentence.

"When's the last time you ate?" Seth asked.

"About this time yesterday."

"I know a little place here in Burlington where you can get a square meal for a quarter. Food's as good as my mama's home cooking."

Just the mention of home-cooked food made my mouth water. I swallowed hard. "I can't leave. I might miss my sister."

"Tell you what, if you give me a little of that money you're hiding who knows where, I could go to the restaurant and bring something back for you."

"Turn your back," I said.

Seth turned, and I unpinned one of the dollar bills from the inside of my camisole.

"Pot roast or ham?" he asked, stuffing my dollar into the same hip pocket where he'd stuffed the train schedule.

"Ham," I answered, thinking it would be less messy for Seth to carry.

And then Seth was gone, and I was alone again, watching the clock. Tick, tick, tick.

The station filled with people and emptied again as a westbound train arrived and then departed. Tick, tick, tick, growl, rumble, tick, tick, tick.

Tick, tick . . . Hannah!

Chapter 5

HANNAH

I DIDN'T RECOGNIZE HANNAH IMMEDIATELY, BECAUSE I WAS NOT EXPECT-
ing her to be wearing men's trousers. "I'm so sorry I'm late,"
Hannah said, gathering me into a hug. Hannah's arms felt like
home, and we both had tears in our eyes when we pulled apart.

"I'll finish my apologies later, truly I will, but we need to get
back to the *Oh My* as quickly as possible." Hannah took up the handle of Mama's carpetbag with one hand and my hand with the
other. I grabbed the empty lunch basket, and we started for the
door. Then I remembered Seth and my dollar.

"I need to—" I began, but stopped myself before the words
wait for my change slipped out. Hannah wouldn't understand. "I need
to send Mama a telegram," I said.

"We can stop by the Western Union window on our way out,"
Hannah replied.

"It's here in the station?"

"Just at the end of that hallway."

I imagined Mama then, waiting and worrying and wringing her hands at the Western Union office back in Prairie Hill. Walking up to the window every few minutes and asking if a telegram had come through from me to her.

I stepped up to the window and asked the man behind the bars for a telegram form, then quickly wrote, "Arrived safely. Hannah here now. Trip long and uneventful. Will write longer letter soon. Megan."

"That'll be a dollar twenty-eight," the telegram man said when he'd counted out the words.

"But . . ."

"Eight cents a word, no exceptions."

I snatched the form back and began marking out words, all the while wondering who it was that had said words were cheap. When I'd finished, the telegram read, "Arrived safely. Letter to follow. Megan."

I'd gone from the wealth of a partway-home railway ticket and two one-dollar bills to a puny fifty-two cents in little more than an hour. I was good at seeing, but I had failed miserably in watching my money.

I carried my carelessness like bricks as Hannah hurried us along, though the weight lifted considerably when I saw what was waiting for us outside—an honest-to-goodness bicycle. I'd seen a few on the streets back home in Prairie Hill, pedaled by town boys, but I hadn't even held out a hope that I'd ever ride on one. "Isaac took it in trade for some cabinetry work," Hannah said, hanging Mama's carpetbag over one of the handlebars and the lunch basket over the other. Hannah gave me a choice: I could ride sidesaddle on the center bar or up front on the handlebars. Sidesaddle was something I knew.

Hannah pushed off and we wobbled forward. I was sure we were going to fall, but the faster Hannah pedaled, the straighter we went. I think there were people on the sidewalks. I think there were wagons and buggies in the street. I say *think*, because I was so busy hoping that one day Hannah might allow me to pedal the bicycle by myself that everything else was a blur. Before turning onto Front Street, we passed over three sets of teeth-chattering iron railway tracks, and I switched from hoping to holding on for dear life.

Front Street opened my eyes. A row of three-story brick buildings towered to our left. Among these were the Northwestern Furniture Company, Pilger's Wholesale Groceries, the Pickle Works, and the City Roller Mill. I kept a lookout for Seth as we bumped along, hoping we'd cross paths so I could at least collect the leftover change from my dollar. And say goodbye. And thank him. And, most importantly, get my hands on that slice of lovely ham.

To the right, the land sloped gently downward until disappearing beneath the skirts of the Mississippi River. Hannah called this the levee. At the water's edge, boats of all shapes and sizes were tied by thick ropes to fat wooden posts. The late afternoon sun threw long, boat-shaped shadows far out into the river—the Mississippi River! A river so wide it deserved all those double letters in its name.

Front Street dead-ended at another triple set of railway tracks, these running north and south. "We'll walk the rest of the way," Hannah said, setting her foot down and bringing the bike to a stop.

"Which boat is the *Oh My*?" I asked as we walked along the levee. I was hoping that it was the last boat in the row. Not the largest, but the one sporting the most gingerbread trim.

"She's tied just around the bend," Hannah answered. And then we were around the bend, and the only thing tied there was a paint-blistered boat, not much wider or longer than Mama's chicken coop. It had a paddlewheel like the others, a smokestack, a rail circling the cluttered deck, but in comparison, Hannah's boat was like a shabby wool sweater that had been left out in the weather too long and had shrunk.

"Oh my," I said.

"Those were my exact words when I first saw her, and that's where Isaac got the name." Hannah squeezed my hand. "I can tell that you're disappointed."

"It's just that I thought she'd be a bit larger."

"Did you read my letters to Mama, the ones where I described her?"

I nodded. I had read those letters, quite some time before. In the meantime, the picture I carried in my head had grown in both size and stature to keep time with the ever-expanding descriptions Mama had used, boasting about the *Oh My* to her friends.

"She's an ugly duckling, to be sure, but she has the heart of a swan. I'm sure you'll grow to love her as much as we do."

"I love her already," I said, hoping that my feelings would match my words sooner or later.

Hannah's expression grew serious then. "Before we go onboard, I need to tell you about Isaac. Thursday, we came upon a tow of floating logs that had begun breaking apart. I steered the *Oh My* alongside, and Isaac jumped off to help. Somehow his leg slipped between two logs. Before he could free himself, the logs shifted, leaving him with a badly injured leg. A doctor in Keokuk wanted to amputate. Isaac wouldn't hear of that, so I'm trying to tend to his wound as best I can. Isaac's a fighter, but he's not out of the woods yet and is still in a great deal of pain. He'll put on a good face, try to make you think that he's doing just fine. I'd like for you to play along, if you don't mind."

If words were knives, few would slash more deeply than "amputation." I wanted to say something to Hannah, about how sorry I was, but all I could manage was a nod.

Chapter 6

THE *OH MY*

A LONG AND NARROW PLANK BRIDGED THE *OH MY* AND THE SHORE. Hannah wheeled the bicycle across with not so much as a wobble. I'd walked the plank only halfway when I made the mistake of looking down and realized the only thing keeping me from the water was my balance. "Don't let the troll trip you up," Hannah called, and that was all I needed.

"You remembered about the troll," I said after I'd planted myself on the *Oh My*'s deck.

Hannah smiled and led me inside. The room we entered was a surprise. The wood-planked walls and ceiling were painted a fresh white. A ladder, seeming to lead nowhere, climbed upward at the room's center. On the wall to the left of the entrance door were two narrow bunks, one above the other and supported by wooden, floor-to-ceiling posts. A window divided the light, half on the upper bunk, half on the lower. The lower bunk was spread with a quilted patchwork of grinning fish. Hannah must have read my thoughts as I stared at the upper bunk wondering how on earth I'd hoist myself up there in a ladylike fashion. "Not to worry," she said, "Jon-Jacob is beside himself with joy that he's graduating to the upper bunk. See there, that extra rail. Isaac added that last week, as a precaution against a middle-of-the-night thump. Jon-Jacob insisted that you use his fish quilt, however, and I added these curtains to the lower bunk, to give you a little privacy."

I gladly unburdened myself of Mama's carpetbag on the fabric pool of fish.

On the wall opposite the bunks, there was a wider, single-layer bed. Like the bunks, this bed was held in place by wooden posts. Unlike the bunks, its window shone undivided light on the intertwined circles of the wedding quilt Mama, my sisters, and I had pieced together for Hannah and Isaac's wedding gift. Time and many washings had, I hoped, removed the droplets of blood I'd shed when my inexperienced hands had jammed the needle, repeatedly, into my seven-year-old fingertips. Curtains, similar to those on the lower bunk, were tied back at the corner posts.

Farther along each of the side walls were another set of windows. Beneath the window on the right, was a dry sink, and next to the dry sink, a small iron cookstove. Lipped shelves, holding dinner plates, cups, glasses, and such, ran along the wall from the stovepipe to the far corner where the shelf made a left turn before running along an inside wall. The shelf ended, temporarily, at a doorway, and then started its run again on the other side, turning yet another corner before ending at the fourth window. This last window looked in across a round table and four mismatched wooden chairs.

"This is lovely," I said to Hannah.

"We like it. Small, yet cozy," she answered.

"Is that Megan Barnett's voice I hear?" Isaac called from somewhere beyond the inside doorway.

"Yes, sir," I answered.

"Well get yourself on in here so I can have a look at you."

I brushed my hands over the wrinkles in Lila's wedding suit and was about to begin tidying my hair when Hannah said, "You look just fine."

We passed through a dim, narrow room, which looked to be a well-stocked pantry, and entered the boiler room. The boiler room was smaller than the living quarters, but larger than the pantry. Occupying much of this space was a full-bellied monstrosity of a thing with a tangle of pipes for arms and sinister gauges for eyes. Isaac sat in a chair next to this beast, his bandaged right leg propped up on a pyramid of cut wood. Isaac was little changed from when I'd last seen him at the wedding. His boyish grin was framed with freckles, and his sandy-colored hair was mussed.

"This can't be Megan," Isaac said, his eyes smiling. "The Megan I remember wasn't much taller than Jon-Jacob. And now look at you, you've turned into a mighty fine young lady."

While I blushed, Hannah lifted the lid on a padded woodbin that was situated beneath one of the boiler room's two windows. She reached inside and out popped Jon-Jacob.

"Say hello to your Auntie Megan," Hannah prompted as she brushed bits of tree bark off Jon-Jacob's knickers.

Jon-Jacob hid his face in Hannah's trouser leg.

"None of that, young man," Isaac scolded.

"I don't mind, sir. He'll come around when he's ready."

"You can drop the sir. Sir is for fathers and older fellows. I've got my hands full being a pa to Jon-Jacob and being laid up already makes me feel as old as Moses. Now tell me, did you have a good trip?"

"Yes, sir . . . I . . . I mean . . . yes, I had a good trip."

"Did Hannah explain that I'm to blame for our getting to Burlington so far behind schedule?"

Hannah stepped forward. "There will be time for explanations later. We need to get under way, else we'll not make it to the island before nightfall."

Isaac raised a hand to his brow, saluted, and said, "Aye, aye, Cap'n."

Hannah leaned over Isaac and kissed him on his forehead.

Jon-Jacob pushed between them, and said, "Aye, aye, Cap'n Mama." Jon-Jacob got a kiss, too.

Getting under way wasn't a simple matter of untying the *Oh My* and pushing off. Isaac had kept the boiler fire going while Hannah had gone into Burlington to fetch me, but there wasn't enough water to build the full head of steam we'd need. Hannah assigned me to one end of a two-ended pump handle and soon a gush of water rose up from the river, through the pipe, and into the boiler's belly. As I pumped, I took a look around. Doors on either outside wall led to the narrow side-decks. On the wall opposite the woodbin was a second window, and beneath this window was what appeared to be a woodworking bench.

We pumped until Jon-Jacob snapped his suspenders with his thumbs and proudly announced that the water gauge had reached the full mark. We left Isaac to tend to the boiler then and made our way back to the cabin, where Hannah suggested that it would probably be best if I changed out of my traveling clothes while we waited for the boiler to reach full-steam. Hannah must have eyed me eyeing for a scrap of privacy. "I'm afraid the pantry is as close as you'll get to privacy on the *Oh My*. I've extra pairs of trousers, on the bottom shelf, if you feel comfortable trying them."

There was barely enough room in the pantry to squeeze me and Mama's carpetbag in sideways, what with the clutter of crates and bulky sacks stacked on the floor and the jars of home-canned food lining rows of narrow shelves—apple butter and preserved beef, carrots and chutney, peaches and pickles and pears. And, beneath a tea towel, hand-embroidered with a wide-eyed owl, lay a lattice-topped cherry pie with three slices remaining. Careful not to drool on Lila's wedding suit, I changed out of the on-loan clothes and into the only choice I was comfortable with—one of my well-worn white shirtwaists and a badly wrinkled brown gabardine skirt. I might have imagined this, but I think my toes sighed when they came to roost inside my everyday shoes. I also might have imagined that pie saying, "Hannah won't miss just one little pinch." When I'd pinched away half of a slice, I licked my fingers, my stomach applauded, and Isaac shouted, "Steam's up."

I hurried into and through the cabin and out onto the deck, thinking I'd confess before Hannah got a whiff of my cherry breath. Hannah was already on the shore. She was barefoot and her trousers were rolled up to just below the knee. "Catch," she said, just before throwing the mooring rope's knotted end at me.

I missed.

Jon-Jacob giggled, then began to drag the sopping rope out of the water. Hannah had only enough time to scurry onboard and pull in the plank behind her before the *Oh My* drifted to more than a plank-length distance from shore. Two planks. Three, and we were surrounded by water. Swirling, churning, dizzying water . . .

"When was the last time you ate a meal?" Hannah asked as she helped me to my feet.

"Yesterday, I think."

"Oh, my. No wonder you're woozy. We'll fix that, right now. Jon-Jacob, be a dear and fetch Auntie Megan something to eat."

"Cherry pie?"

"Oh my, no. Too much sweetness on an empty stomach will only make matters worse. Bring a couple of the leftover breakfast biscuits."

"Aye, aye, Cap'n Mama." Jon-Jacob saluted.

Hannah guided me to a backless bench that was set against the outside wall of the cabin. "How thoughtless of me. I should have asked if you were hungry the minute you came aboard. You have to tell us when you need something."

"Mama said I'm not to be a bother."

Hannah brushed a stray strand of hair off my forehead. "You could never be a bother, Megan! Truth be told, you're a godsend."

"She's drifting," Isaac shouted from the boiler room.

It took me a moment to realize that Isaac wasn't referring to me.

Hannah stood. "I need to get us moving upriver. We're not going far today, so it won't take long. Meantime just ask Jon-Jacob to fetch whatever you need."

Cold biscuits never tasted so grand, though my last bite caught in my throat when the *Oh My*'s roaring whistle blasted the quiet. Jon-Jacob fetched me a dipper of water from the nearby rain barrel. I'd just taken a sip when the boat groaned, shuddered, and began making a loud slapping sound. "What's that?" I asked.

46

"Paddlewheel. Do you like toads?"

"Well, that depends. If it's a toad that causes warts, then no, I'm not at all fond of those. But if it's a toad that turns into a handsome prince when kissed, well, I wouldn't mind making its acquaintance."

Jon-Jacob fished a small toad out of his pocket and thrust it under my nose. "This one's a prince," he said, grinning.

I passed Jon-Jacob's test, though the toad failed to turn into a prince. "How about garter snakes?" Jon-Jacob then asked.

"You don't have one in your pocket, do you?"

"Naw, but I almost caught one the day Papa smashed his leg." Jon-Jacob opened both hands and then slammed them together. "Logs, you know."

"Oh my."

Jon-Jacob got a puzzled look on his face. "You talk just like my mama."

"That's because we're sisters."

"I had a sister once. Mama let me look at her before they closed the box. She wasn't any bigger than a pup. When it gets dark, I'll show you the star she lives on. It's the brightest one."

We were both sitting there, our heads craned skyward, imagining, I suppose, when Hannah's voice drifted down from above. "Megan, are you feeling better?"

"Much better, thank you," I called back.

"Join me then. Jon-Jacob will show you the way."

The wheelhouse was reached by climbing the ladder inside the cabin. At the top was a shoulder-wide square opening that was covered by a hinged door. I lifted this door with my head because I was afraid I'd fall off the ladder if I let go with either hand. Glass wrapped all four sides of the wheelhouse. In the weeks to come, I'd seek out the view whenever I could. That day all I could see on three sides was too much water, so I focused on the fourth. The fourth, which contained not only windows but a door, looked out on a rooftop farm. The roof-farm was surrounded by a railing much like on the lower deck, except that it was filled in from bottom to top with chicken wire. Dirt-filled oblong flats rimmed the roof's edge. Rooted in the dirt, young vegetable plants bathed in the sun. Three Rock Island Red laying hens pecked at a pan of cracked corn. A fourth hen peeked out from within a small wooden coop.

Chickens I knew. "Who gathers the eggs?" I asked.

"That's my job," Jon-Jacob answered, pride plumping both his chest and his voice.

"And a mighty fine egg gatherer you are," Hannah said, pride plumping her voice too.

"The only thing missing is a milk cow, though I suppose it would be hard to coax one up the ladder," I said.

"Exactly!" Hannah answered.

I stayed in the wheelhouse only until Hannah spotted a suitable island. Suitable, she told me, meant a sandy and relatively deep-water shore. Sandiness could be measured with the eyes. Measuring the water depth was more involved. And risky. Though she was flatbottomed, the *Oh My* required at least two feet of water beneath her to prevent scraping, and possibly, as Jon-Jacob demonstrated with his hands, ripping a hole in the hull or splintering one of the paddles on the paddlewheel.

The paddlewheel slapping slow, I leaned over the deck rail and stabbed at the water with a long bamboo pole that was marked with colored bands. When the pole's tip hit mud, I called the marks up to Hannah in the wheelhouse. One mark showed, then two, then three before the *Oh My*'s nose nudged the shore.

Hannah was on deck and over the side quicker than I could ask what on earth I should do next. "Throw me the mooring rope," she said, standing in water that licked the rolls of her trouser legs.

I missed, and Hannah had to wade into waist-deep water to fetch the knot.

"Sorry."

"You'll get the hang of it. All you need is a little practice."

Sunset had painted the sky a velvety pink by the time Hannah had tied the *Oh My* to a sturdy tree near the shore. After more than thirty-six hours of swaying trains and bottom-bruising bicycle bars and slapping, shuddering paddlewheels, the island felt wonderfully fixed. Solid. Safe.

Chapter 7

THE ISLAND

AFTER WE'D EATEN A SUPPER OF WARMED-OVER NAVY BEAN AND HAM hock soup and divided the last of the pie, Hannah asked me to take Jon-Jacob for a walk while she changed Isaac's bandages. Holding Jon-Jacob's small hand in mine, we strolled along a narrow stretch of sand at the river's edge. A river-scented breeze wove fingers of coolness through the night air. Frogs croaked. Crickets chirruped. Owls hooted. A silvery fish flip-flopped on the river's surface, causing ripples to spread across the moonlit water.

Jon-Jacob scanned the sky for his sister's star. The moon was too bright, so he picked up a rock and heaved it. Plunk. Then another and another. Plunk, plunk. There was something so satisfying in this sound that soon I was heaving and plunking rocks, too. My rocks didn't fly very far, though, so I asked Jon-Jacob what I was doing wrong. He put his hands on his hips and said, "Everything." The secret, he said, was in the letting go, and soon I was sending rocks far out into the river. I did worry about conking a fish in the head, but not enough to stop.

Then a shadow bird swooped across the sky, and then another and another. One flew so close I instinctively ducked. I asked Jon-Jacob what sort of birds they were, and he said they weren't birds but bats, and I said it was time we hightailed it back to the boat. He dragged his feet, so I bribed him with an offer of riding piggyback. Jon-Jacob was heavier than he looked.

Hannah was waiting for us on the *Oh My*'s deck. She gave Jon-Jacob a hug and then told him it was time to get ready for bed and if he was quick about it, his papa would tell him a story. Jon-Jacob ran.

I yawned.

Hannah wrapped an arm around my shoulder. "Let's save our chat for morning, when you're rested."

I didn't fuss, and I didn't take long getting into my nightshirt and into my bunk. On the other side of my curtain, Isaac was in the middle of the story he was telling Jon-Jacob—something about alligators. Beneath me, the *Oh My* rocked gently.

Morning Edition

June 28, 1896

ESCAPEE SPOTTED IN BURLINGTON

BURLINGTON, IOWA—An escapee from the Fort Madison Jail is thought to have been in Burlington yesterday. Local law enforcement, after receiving a dispatch regarding the Fort Madison jailbreak, made some inquiries around town, and Mr. Hatcher, the ticket agent at the Burlington and Missouri Station, recalls redeeming a railway ticket for a young man who fits the escapee's description. The escapee, Samuel Silver, residence unknown, is believed to have been traveling with a young female accomplice. The young woman wore a matronly traveling suit, a navy blue hat, and had in her possession a carpetbag and wicker lunch basket. Citizens are asked to report additional sightings of this pair to the Burlington Constable's office.

Chapter 8

A DAY OF REST?

I AWOKE THE NEXT MORNING TO JON-JACOB'S SHOUT. "MAMA, I THINK Auntie Megan is dead!"

My eyelids flew open to Jon-Jacob's grin. He stepped away and let my privacy curtain fall back into place. "Naw, you were right, Mama, she was only sleeping."

"Didn't I tell you not to wake Auntie Megan?" Hannah scolded just before lifting the corner of my curtain.

"What time is it?" I asked, rubbing the sleep from my eyes.

"Nearly noon."

Impossible. I'd never slept past six o'clock in my life. Mama, with her "early birds get the worm," had always seen to that. "You should have wakened me!"

"We've decided to lay over here on the island for a couple of days, to give Isaac's leg a chance to heal, so there wasn't a reason to wake you."

"But you must have some work that I can do. That's why I came, and now I've slept away half of my first day."

"Nonsense. On the *Oh My* we take life as it comes. We sleep when we're tired; eat when we're hungry. And when we need a break, we take one."

"Speaking of hungry," Isaac said from somewhere in the cabin. "I'm famous for my flapjacks."

"Don't go to any trouble for me," I answered back.

"No trouble. I'm not much good for anything else with this bum leg of mine, so you have to humor me into thinking that I'm being useful."

Later, after I'd washed up and dressed, I sat myself down at the table and Isaac, who was balancing on his crutch, flipped a perfectly tanned and freckled flapjack onto my plate. "When we get up to Minnesota, we can trade for some real maple syrup. Until then, you'll have to make do with a smear of this clover honey. Hannah harvested the comb, snatched it from the hole in a rotted tree before the bees even knew she was there."

"Mama can run like all get out," Jon-Jacob added.

Hannah ruffled Jon-Jacob's hair. "I have to run fast to keep up with you."

I ate two flapjacks, barely taking a breath in between. Jon-Jacob, leaning his elbows on the table, watched every bite enter my mouth. When I finally lay down my fork, he turned to Hannah. "Auntie Megan's done eating. Can we go into the woods now?"

Within the hour Hannah, Jon-Jacob, and I were tramping through the woods on the island. Hannah pushed a wheelbarrow upon which was balanced a two-handled crosscut saw, an ax, and a splitting maul, and within which rested a jug of water and a gathering basket. We were searching for a fallen, though rot-free, tree, and when we didn't find one right away, we fanned out. The closest I'd ever come to being in the woods was a stand of thinly spaced cottonwood trees that lined the banks of Lincoln Creek back in Nebraska. The trees on the island grew so closely together that only winks of daylight made their way to the forest floor, which walked soft with damp leaves and nettles. Lacy ferns fingered my skirts. Birds, which I'd later learn were jays, cardinals, goldfinches, orioles, and a host of others, threaded color against the green as if a delicate crochet work. Mosquitoes swarmed, but few alighted because I'd heeded Hannah's warning and slathered my hands and face with a concoction of vinegar and citronella oil. Though the forest smelled like earth-scented rain, I smelled like pickled lemons.

I was the first to find a likely tree. I'd been staring upward instead of watching where I was going and tripped over its thick trunk.

Hannah, hearing my squeal, arrived just as I'd gotten back to my feet. "It's perfect. Oak is one of the best woods because it burns long and hot."

I'd never cut wood before. On the farm, which had few trees, we burned corncobs in the cookstove. "The secret is in the rhythm," Hannah said as she positioned the blade of the crosscut saw over the wrist of a branch. I wrapped my hands around the handle at the other end, and Hannah pushed the saw in my direction. I pushed back and the blade chattered across the craggy bark. We lifted the blade back into the scar Hannah's pass had made and tried again. That time the blade stayed put. Back and forth, sawdust raining down about our feet. Sawdust that made me think of Horace and his doors. Was he, like me, looking for familiar shapes in the grain of the wood or in the hills and valleys of the bark? Were his arms aching from the back and forth of the saw?

"Tell me about your trip," Hannah said.

"It was long."

"Did you meet any interesting characters?"

"A few," I answered. I was afraid that Hannah might spill the beans to Mama about my spending time with strange men, so I told her about Mrs. Galt and her ailment machine, and, thinking Mama wouldn't mind if I'd spent time with a preacher, I told Hannah about the Reverend Herman.

"You should be proud of yourself, Megan. Many people, people a lot older than you, aren't brave enough to travel alone, and it sounds like you made the best of it."

"I was so brave I thought for a while of getting off the train and returning home."

"I'm grateful that you chose to continue on. With Isaac laid up, we'd be in a real fix . . . watch your feet."

The saw broke through the bottom of the branch just then and fell to the ground with what would have been a toe-crushing thud. We stretched our backs, mopped our brows, and then moved the blade up the branch's arm and started in sawing again.

As we worked, Hannah asked me to tell her the news from back home. I chattered on about Mama and Alice bickering, and about how Joey had decided that if he couldn't attend the high school in Prairie Hill when he finished the eighth grade, he was planning to run away and join the French Foreign Legion.

"How does Papa feel about Joey going to high school?" Hannah asked.

"You know Papa."

"And Mama?"

"Mama's secretly saving a little of her egg money each week, so, when the time comes, there'll be enough to pay Joey's room and board."

"Good for Mama, but how about you? Wouldn't you like to go to high school, too?"

"Mama doesn't have that many chickens."

Hannah laughed and was about to say something more on the subject of high school when Jon-Jacob appeared. "Are these the kind that are safe to eat?" he asked, reaching into his gathering basket and lifting out a mushroom.

We stopped sawing, and Hannah inspected the mushrooms carefully. "Yes, these are safe to eat. If you can find even more, we'll cook them up for our supper."

Jon-Jacob rubbed a circle over his stomach, and said, "Mmm-mmm," and then was off.

"He's quite a young man," I said.

"I'm so proud of him. Actually, he reminds me of you when you were his age. Eyes bright with curiosity."

I figured she had me mixed up with Joey, but I'd had so much experience being mixed up with one or the other of my sisters or brothers, I didn't bother to correct her.

As we worked, I came close to telling Hannah about the stolen railway ticket. The words would be right there on the tip of my tongue, but I could never bring myself to let them out. *Hannah has enough to worry about with Isaac's leg,* I reasoned to myself.

By the end of that first afternoon, Hannah and I had sawed, split, hauled, and stacked in the bin enough wood to keep the *Oh My* steaming upriver for only a couple of days. The saw handle had blistered my palms, and I'd perspired so profusely that Hannah's mosquito repellent had given up. Crops of itchy bite bumps dotted any skin that was not covered by clothing. If cutting wood was Hannah's idea of "taking a break," I wondered what spending a day on the river would be like.

Chapter 9

RAIN

RAIN GAVE MY BLISTERS AND MOSQUITO BITES TIME TO HEAL. DRUM-
ming, gray rain that began in the middle of the night and continued
without letup through our second day tied to the island, and into
the third. To take the chill out of the air inside the *Oh My*, Hannah
fired up the cookstove, and, so as not to let all that lovely heat go to
waste, we mixed and kneaded three loaves of bread, rolled out crusts
for one mincemeat and one cherry pie, the aroma of which masked
the musky river scent of the air. To take the drum out of the air,
Hannah and I talked and talked. Mostly we talked about the plan
for the summer. The rehearsals for her play were scheduled to begin
on July 15, so, if all went well, our trip upriver to St. Paul, Minnesota,
would be a leisurely one. Once we arrived in St. Paul, we'd be guests
at the home of a Mr. Thomas Wallencott III, the son of the play's

director, Mr. Thomas Wallencott II. Like Hannah and Isaac, Mr. Wallencott II wintered in New Orleans. When Hannah learned from a friend of a friend that he was looking for a housekeeper, she applied for the job and was immediately hired. Leaving Jon-Jacob in the care of Isaac's mother, Hannah dusted and scrubbed, laundered and baked, and, after a week, cleverly left the script of a play she had written on Mr. Wallencott's nightstand. When she arrived for work the next morning, Mr. Wallencott was waiting at the back door for her, and demanding to know the name and whereabouts of the brilliant, though unpolished, author. Hannah confessed, and so began the relationship between the two. Hannah had stayed on as his housekeeper, and also as his student. By spring, Mr. Wallencott, who was under contract to write and direct two summer plays for a theater group in St. Paul, had finished only one of his own, and so had submitted Hannah's play as the second and had disguised the fact that she was a woman by identifying H. Bradshaw as the play's author. Both plays had been approved, with the most enthusiastic comments coming H. Bradshaw's way.

Hannah would be paid ten percent of the ticket sales. "If it flops," Hannah had said, "I won't make enough to pay for the trolley fare to and from the theater. If it's a hit and held over for the full ten-day run, I might need the wheelbarrow to haul all the cash."

Hannah wouldn't tell me what her play was about, because she wanted me to be surprised when I attended the opening performance.

She did tell me one thing she hadn't told Jon-Jacob. There was a role in her play for a young boy, and she'd asked Mr. Wallencott to request that the role be saved for the playwright's son. "Time would pass too slowly for him if he knew," she'd said. "Way too slowly."

As I listened, I wondered how it could be that Hannah and I had been born into the same family, slept in the same bed, gotten our education at the same country school. Hannah, who was good at things I didn't even know existed, and me, who was good at next to nothing.

Isaac spent most of the rain time asleep. When he was awake, he and Jon-Jacob played checkers and dominos and tiddlywinks, a new game that Hannah said was all the rage in New Orleans. When not playing games, Jon-Jacob drew pictures. Of me! My eyes were so big they took up half my face, my hair stuck out like lightning strikes, and my ears were growing out of my neck. I held the drawings against my heart and told him that I loved them.

Evening Edition

June 30, 1896

CORPS ISSUES WARNING

ST. PAUL, MINNESOTA—The Army Corps of Engineers has issued a warning to riverboat pilots on the Upper Mississippi. Due to heavy rains and rising river levels, pilots should be on the lookout for a goodly number of snags and other floating debris.

RIVER FISHING

THE RAIN FINALLY LET UP IN THE LATE MORNING OF OUR THIRD DAY ON the island, and it was back into the woods for more blisters and mosquito bites. By late afternoon, Hannah and I had sawed and split what Hannah judged to be "quite enough wood for one day."

When we returned to the *Oh My,* Isaac was sitting on a chair at the deck rail. Jon-Jacob was standing at Isaac's side. Both held bamboo fishing poles, their lines dangling into the water. Both wore dilapidated, wide-brimmed straw hats. If someone wanted to paint a picture that said "father and son," that would have been it.

When we'd stacked the next to the last load of wood on the narrow side deck outside the boiler room, Jon-Jacob asked Hannah if he couldn't "please" have a ride in the wheelbarrow.

"But who will keep me company?" Isaac asked, pretending disappointment.

"Auntie Meagan," Jon-Jacob answered, handing me his fishing pole.

I looked to Hannah.

She was of no help at all. She plucked the straw hat off Jon-Jacob's head and plopped it on mine. "That's a capital idea."

So there I was, alone with Isaac for the first time, holding a fishing pole for the first time, and chewing my lip while trying to think of something to say. "Having any luck?" was what I finally settled on.

"Naw, but you should have seen the one that got away. River catfish. Must have weighed twenty pounds."

I tightened my grip on the pole. "How will I know if I've caught a fish?"

"Keep an eye on that cork bobber there, and when it wiggles, that means you've got a nibble. Rear back on the pole and that'll set the hook. Once the fish takes the hook, all you have to do is land it."

"Land it?"

"Sorry. Landing a fish means getting it onboard. Don't worry, if you catch one, I'll talk you through it."

I stared at the bobber, willing it not to wiggle. And it didn't, for the first minute or two. But then . . .

"Pull back," Isaac said, trying to corral the excitement in his voice.

I pulled. The fish pulled even harder, and the tip of the pole arched downward until nearly piercing the water.

"You've got a big one. Whatever you do, don't let go."

I didn't let go, not even when the fish pulled so hard my arms were jerked out over the deck rail. Not even when I braced my hips hard against that same rail. Not even when I heard the sound of cracking, splintering wood. I did, however, let go when I hit the water.

Water swallowed me as if into the belly of Jonah's whale, dark and cool. My body knew not to breathe. Knew that air was up. *UP.* But I couldn't get there. Something was tying up my arms. I tried to punch free, claw my way up to air. My head thumped against something solid. Down, then. Up must be down. No. Down is sandy mud. Lungs bursting. Trapped, trapped, trapped. *Mama was right. I'm too young to travel alone. Too young to die.* Thrashing, not mine. Something tightened strong about my arm. I was moving. Sideways first, then up. Sputtering blue air. Blessed, breathable air. Overhead, the glad, green leaves of an overhanging tree.

"Can you stand?"

I straightened my back and legs, my shoes found bottom, and shockingly, the river rose only as high as my ribs. The grip on my arm loosened. I turned. To see Isaac!

"If you're up to it, I think I'm going to need some help getting out of the water," Isaac said then. His voice was as pale as his face. He used my shoulder as he would a crutch. He'd hop on his good leg toward the shore, grimace, and then hop again. Finally out of the water, he took a few more hops, then lowered himself to the sand and told me I'd best get Hannah.

My wet skirts clung to my ankles, and my shoes sloshed as I ran.

* * *

Getting Isaac onboard the *Oh My* was more difficult than getting him out of the water. With both Hannah and I supporting Isaac from either side, the three of us had to sidestep our way up the boarding plank. Inch our way up, really. Once inside, Isaac collapsed onto his bed. Jon-Jacob tried to climb onto the bed, too, but Hannah held him back. "I need you to help Auntie Megan make a fire in the cookstove, so she can boil water for tea." She nodded to me and then closed the privacy curtain.

Hoping to distract Jon-Jacob, to distract myself, I talked nonstop to Jon-Jacob while I fed kindling to the stove's firebox, filled a kettle with water from the rain barrel, and waited for the water to boil. I asked Jon-Jacob if he thought fish ever wished they could live inside a boat, not underneath it. I asked him if he thought fish mamas and papas gave their fish babies names. Jon-Jacob didn't answer my questions. He was too busy watching Hannah duck in and out of the curtain.

Wet clothes, out—dry clothes, in. Scissors, in—soggy bandages, out. Clean bandages, in—Isaac's howl, out.

"Have you ever heard a fish yodel?" I asked Jon-Jacob, just as Hannah pulled the curtain aside. Isaac's eyes reached across the cabin.

"Papa, Papa," Jon-Jacob shouted.

Isaac opened his arms and Jon-Jacob climbed in. Hannah sat on the edge of the bed beside them. "My wonderful, handsome men," she said, tenderly and by turns, kissing their foreheads and cheeks. I slipped out to the deck and sat my shivers down on the bench. I tried to warm myself by crossing and rubbing my arms. The shivers only deepened, and all that was left for me to do was cry. Frightened tears or relief tears or guilty tears, it didn't matter, and I couldn't have stopped them even if I'd known which kind they were.

I was still shivering and sniveling when, a short while later, Hannah joined me on the bench. "Isaac would like a word with you," she said.

I rose, and, before walking my dread through the door, I looked back. I saw Mama there, in the way Hannah had her elbows propped on her knees, her face in her hands, the exact pose Mama always took when she'd reached her last straw.

Isaac managed a smile. "Change into some dry duds, then come back and we'll talk about our little swimming party."

Dry felt cozy, though I couldn't towel the fishiness from my skin or force a comb through my river-snarled hair. My shoes were hopelessly waterlogged, so I went to talk to Isaac in my stocking feet.

He asked Jon-Jacob to go out and keep his mama company and asked me to pull a chair up next to his bed. When I was sitting, he began. "What happened today wasn't your fault. I hope you know that."

"But—"

"But, nothing. I should have repaired that rotting deck rail months ago. I'm a carpenter, and that's what carpenters are supposed to do."

"I should have let go of the fishing pole."

"I told you not to."

"The water wasn't that deep. I should have been able to save myself."

"Do you know why you couldn't?"

"I panicked?"

"No. You couldn't find your way up because you got trapped beneath the boat. Likely as not, your skirts got twisted in the pieces of broken rail, and when you tried to free yourself, you slipped under the hull. Long skirts and rivers are a bad mix."

Suddenly it all made sense, the way I'd bumped my head on what I'd thought should have been air. And then, just as suddenly, I remembered that I hadn't thanked Isaac for diving in after me.

I was in the middle of thanking him, of saying how sorry I was that he'd reinjured his leg in the process, when Isaac interrupted.

"No thanks necessary. I'd save my worst enemy if he were drowning. I didn't have to think twice about going in for my favorite sister-in-law. Besides, your pa's never been real fond of me. If I'd have let you drown, he'd probably come here himself and hang me by my toenails from the nearest tree."

"Papa wouldn't do that."

"I was just making light."

"Oh."

In the letter I wrote to Mama that night, I made no mention of my river baptism. I made no mention of Isaac's injured leg. I made no mention of the stolen railway ticket or that my bloomers were flying like flags from the rooftop clothesline for everyone on the river to see. I wrote quite a lot about Jon-Jacob, and I did mention that I was getting lots of fresh air and exercise.

Chapter 22

MOVING UPRIVER

BY THE TIME THE SUN PEEKED OVER THE BLUFF TOPS ON THE EASTERN
shore, we were steaming upriver. Though Hannah thought Isaac
looked a little pale, he'd insisted that he felt fine and could handle
his boiler room duties—if I'd consider becoming his apprentice. I
readily agreed. In comparison to mother's helper, with its dirty
floors and dirty diapers, boiler-room apprentice rang of important
work. Dirty was part of it, though. And muggy hot.

And an awesome responsibility. Reading the gauges was the most
tricky. Too little steam and the *Oh My* would lose power and drift.
Too much steam in the boiler and it would explode, which would
mean the end of us all. And then there were the bells, three in all,
attached by cords to the wheelhouse. One for full speed ahead, one
for half, and one for stop. Forgetting which was which could spell

disaster. The engine, which was located between the boiler and the back wall of the boat, housed a piston, which was connected to a bulky iron yoke, which was connected to the Pitman arm, which drove the paddlewheel, was less of a worry. Isaac would say, "It purrs like a kitten." *Purr* wasn't the word I would have used. The chuffing of each piston stroke was more like that of an angry bull's snort.

Isaac mixed the *Oh My*'s history in with his boiler-room lessons. She'd had many lives. A weekend pleasure boat for a wealthy banker in New Orleans. A floating office for one of the higher-ups with the Corps of Engineers, and finally a ferry transporting ordinary folks who wanted to get from one side of the river to the other. She'd been treated poorly by the fellow who used her as a ferry, and by the time she'd been towed into Gluck's Boatworks, where Isaac worked winters as a carpenter, her hull was riddled with wood rot, her paddlewheel was missing two of its paddles, and her boiler had rusted through. Isaac had known, the minute he saw her, that she had "good bones" and that she'd make the perfect home for Hannah and him, after they were married. Mr. Gluck had driven a hard bargain, though. He'd trade the wreck of a boat for the fine skiff Isaac had built from the ribs up. "I sure hated to let go of *Hannah's Fair Wind,* it being the boat that had gotten me and my ma away from Prairie Hill and away from my good-for-nothing step-father. But *Hannah's Fair Wind* wasn't a boat you could live in, wasn't a boat you could raise a family in, so I shook hands on it, and spent the next year making the *Oh My* river-worthy. I was just getting to the work of making her pretty when Hannah sent word that her pa had given his permission for us to marry. I dropped everything and hopped on the next train heading toward Nebraska. So she wasn't much to look at when I carried Hannah over her threshold. And I guess she's not much to look at now. We'll get her painted up on the outside, one of these years, but, like Hannah always says, beauty comes from the heart, not the covering."

Talking with Isaac was like talking with Horace—grown-up and friendly. Not like back home where men never went out of their way to talk to girls in the first place, and when they did, they'd talk to you like you were three feet tall and five years old.

Jon-Jacob, who had spent his morning running messages back and forth between Hannah and Isaac, appeared at the door a little before eleven. "I'm awful hungry, and Mama says, if I ask nice and polite, maybe you'll fix me some lunch."

I looked to Isaac, and he excused me with an approving nod. In the cabin, I called up to Hannah to ask what she'd planned. "Whatever you're hungry for will be fine," she'd answered back.

When I asked Jon-Jacob what he was hungry for, he wasn't shy about sharing. He wanted hush puppies, and when I told him I didn't know what those were, he said, "Okay, I want jambalaya." When I shook my head to that, he asked, "What *do* you know how to cook?"

"Nebraska food."

GALWAY COUNTY LIBRARIES

"What's that?"

"It's the kind of food your mama and papa ate before they moved to Louisiana."

"Okay, then, make me a plate of Nebraska food. I'm starving."

I rooted around in the pantry, scared up the ingredients I'd need—bacon, rolled oats, brown sugar, raisins, cinnamon, cloves—and whipped up a big batch of fried oatmeal.

I served Jon-Jacob first, then carried a plate to Isaac and another, carefully and one-handed, up the ladder to Hannah in the wheelhouse. By the time I sat down at the table, Jon-Jacob had cleaned his plate and was staring wide-eyed at mine. "Still hungry?" I asked.

He nodded. "My tummy sure wants some more of that Nebraska food."

Hannah invited me up to the wheelhouse after lunch, saying that I probably needed a break from the commotion of the boiler room. She was right. When under way, the wheelhouse was the quietest place on the *Oh My.* And the coolest. Window breezes didn't have to squabble with fireboxes and steam for space.

Beyond the windows, the river. An American bald eagle soared overhead. Lushly treed bluffs, resembling the humped backs of huddled green cows, rose and valleyed along the far shore. On the near shore, a cluster of houses soaked their toes at the river's edge.

Hannah brought an abrupt end to my seeing when she asked, "Are you ready for your first piloting lesson?"

I answered with the first thing that came to my buzzing head. "But I can't swim."

Hannah was quiet for a moment, like she was having trouble putting one thing together with the other, then said, "Okay, then you'll have your piloting lesson now and a swimming lesson tonight."

For fear that Hannah had even more lessons up her sleeve, I stepped forward, swallowed the tremble in my voice, and asked, "You won't leave, will you?"

"No, of course not. I just want you to get the feel of the wheel. With Isaac's leg injured, he can't manage the ladder, so I'll be the pilot for the rest of the trip, but if something should happen to me, you'll need to know enough to step in and steer her safely to shore. Lesson one—the wheel is attached by wires to the rudder. The rudder is like a fish's fin and is attached to the underside of the boat near the back, or stern. If you turn the wheel left, which is also called port, the rudder swings to the right or starboard side."

I'd never been particularly good at left and right, especially in a panic, which I expected would be the case if I were ever called upon to pilot the *Oh My* solo. The fried oatmeal turned to stone in my stomach as I wrapped my hands around the wheel.

"Easy now. Less is always better than more when you're steering."

I managed to keep the *Oh My* moving ahead, managed to keep

the bobbing red channel markers to the right and the green to the left as Hannah instructed. And then we came to a bend in the river—and steaming around the bend was an enormous, fast-moving riverboat.

"Permission to relieve Cap'n Megan?" Hannah said.

"Oh, yes, please."

Hannah stepped in, I out, and it took several shakes to rid the ache of responsibility from my hands.

Though Hannah was still learning the river herself, she tried her best to teach me what she knew. Traffic was the first item on Hannah's what-to-look-out-for list. Getting out of traffic's way, that is. As with the chickens in the henhouse back home, there was a pecking order on the river. Smaller boats were expected to get out of the way of the larger ones, especially the bulky barges. Few boats on the river were smaller than the *Oh My*, so Hannah steered out of the way quite a lot.

Second on the list was a class of dangers that were, in many cases, hard to see—dangers that could sink the *Oh My*. Dead trees, which Hannah called snags. Some snags floated on the surface and could be dealt with either by steering wide or, as was the case that afternoon, by me going down to the deck of the *Oh My*, leaning over the rail, and nudging the menacing trunk out of the way with the measuring pole. It was the submerged snags, caught up in the silt, that posed the greatest threat. Passing over one of these could rip a gash in the *Oh My*'s hull. If that happened, we'd sink.

Snags weren't the only sinking hazards. There were jagged boulders and hulks of old riverboats that had sunk after hitting snags or boulders or after their boilers had exploded. Submerged sandbars weren't as risky as snags. If you hit one, your boat would become high-centered, which was the opposite of sunk. If you got stuck instead of sunk, then you'd have to wait for hours, days even, for a friendly towboat captain to go out of his way to pull you out of your predicament. The government had a small fleet of snag boats, their job being to keep the channel clear. The problem was that because the *Oh My* had to steer clear of the larger boats, including the snag boats, we spent a good part of that afternoon hugging the channel's edge, which was where the danger from snags and sandbars was the greatest.

A good eye, Hannah had said, could mean the difference between being sunk or stuck or going on our merry way. The secret was in learning to read the water. A sunken obstacle, like a snag or a riverboat carcass, caused the water to hump in gurgling whorls. A sandbar caused ripples. Wind blowing downstream also caused ripples, though if one looked closely enough, the wind ripples glimmered more than the sandbar ripples. Reading ripples, it seemed, was like reading winks—you had a hunch what they meant, but could never be perfectly sure.

The yellowed, edge-curled navigation charts, which Hannah consulted frequently, marked the known sinking hazards and mapped the river's main channel, which was as crooked as a side-winding snake. One bend would point due north and the next west or east, and on the rare twist briefly south. In some places the river stretched unhindered from shore to shore; in others, it wended its way through a maze of islands. In some places the channel hugged Iowa, in others it preferred Illinois. The Mississippi seemed to be a river that couldn't quite make up its mind.

These charts weren't completely reliable, however. "The river is like us," Hannah said. "It's ever changing. New sandbars can form overnight. Boulders, some as large as a house, can break away from the face of the bluff and plummet into the river. And there's not a year goes by without a handful of boat carcasses being added to the river graveyard."

The more I learned, the more I worried and the more I wondered why Hannah and Isaac had chosen such a dangerous life. "Why not just stay in New Orleans year-round, or move back to Nebraska, where it's safe?" I asked at a point where the river's surface rippled, seemingly from shore to shore.

"There's no place that's safe," Hannah answered, tugging the cord of the half-speed-ahead bell. "Louisiana has hurricanes. In Nebraska, there are blizzards, tornados, and prairie fires. You know as well as I the hazards Papa and Mama face on the farm. Someone falling under the wheel of the wagon or being gored by a bull. We choose to spend our summers on the river because the river is where we feel most free and, more importantly, most alive."

I thought long and hard about that, and came to the conclusion that Hannah might be on to something. If aliveness were measured by the number of times my heart had thumped to danger's frenzied beat that day, then, yes, I was feeling more alive than would probably be considered healthy.

DR. MILLER TO ATTEND SON'S WEDDING

ROCK ISLAND, ILLINOIS—Dr. Matthew Miller will not be seeing patients in the next twelve days as he and his lovely wife, Annabell, will leave on the morning train for Chicago, where they will attend the wedding of their son, Matthew Jr., to Miss Julia Waters, the daughter of a prominent Chicago banker. In case of emergency, patients should call upon Dr. Hale.

Chapter 12

MUSCATINE

BY TWO-THIRTY THAT AFTERNOON, HANNAH DECIDED TO CALL IT A day. We moored the *Oh My* within walking distance of the city of Muscatine, though Hannah had a difficult time finding a stretch of shore that wasn't already occupied by clusters of clammers' tents. "Clammers," as Hannah explained, were people who harvested mussels from the river bottom and sold the shells to pearl-button factories in Muscatine.

Hannah was busy tending to Isaac's leg, and Jon-Jacob had struck up a friendship with a young boy from a nearby camp, so I would be alone in finding my way to the post office, to mail my letter to Mama. I brushed a day's worth of worry and work from my hair and removed my soot-soiled apron before setting off for town. Thankfully, there was a well-worn footpath that followed a single set of railway tracks. A path littered with broken shells, and at one point, wolf whistles. Not thinking, I looked back over my shoulder. Two men in the camp I'd just passed grinned back at me. My cheeks flamed as I hurried on.

The Muscatine levee, much like the one in Burlington, was crowded with towers of lumber, crates, barrels, stray dogs, and all manner of people. Looking through Mama's eyes, I chose a well-dressed older man to ask directions to the post office. He tipped his hat, smiled, and said, "It would be my pleasure to escort you there myself." He then offered his elbow. At a loss for how to politely refuse, I slipped my arm in his and off we went. Elbow man didn't tell me his name, or ask for mine, though he was quite chatty. In the three blocks it took for him to escort me to the post office steps, I learned that he made his living as an undertaker and, it being such a fine day, he'd decided to take a break from his work for an afternoon stroll. The thought of what he did with his elbow when not entwined, too tightly, with mine caused my skin to creep. His undertaking parlor was in his home, which he shared with his wife, and, when they were growing up, his five daughters. The daughters, much to his distress, had all married and moved away. It didn't take much imagination to understand why. *I sure know how to pick them,* I thought.

I believe the undertaker would have followed me inside the post office if not for some long-overdue quick thinking on my part. I told him that I would be inside for quite a while, finishing my letter before mailing it. He wished me a good day and, I suppose, returned to whatever dead body he'd been tending before taking his afternoon stroll.

And I *was* inside the post office for quite a while, though not for the reason I'd given the undertaker. After spending two of my remaining fifty-two cents on a postage stamp, my eyes were drawn to bold dollar signs printed on posters that lined one wall. WANTED posters! Murderers, bank robbers, and horse thieves. The $200 posters displayed printed photographs of the wanted men. I studied and memorized every facial detail, though their evil eyes staring back at me caused one of my eyelids to twitch. The $100 posters didn't have photographs, but painted the criminals with words—height, weight, body build, unusual scars, tattoos, habits. One walked with a limp; another talked of nothing but horses.

And then, as I was standing there, a man tacked a new poster to the wall.

Fort Madison Escapee

Samuel Silver. 5 feet 8 inches tall, 140 to 150 pounds, 21 years old. Brown hair, short beard, is boyish looking and has very white teeth. Talks a great deal. Has a dancing girl tattooed on his right forearm. Gambler by profession. Last seen in Burlington, Iowa.

I read it. Memorized it, wondered why there was no reward money listed. Apparently this Samuel Silver fellow wasn't worth a penny.

In the weeks to come, I'd keep an eye out for the wanted men who had a price on their heads, and I began searching at once. As I strolled Muscatine that afternoon, I paid closest attention to those men whose clothing was tattered or hair was uncombed or had a general look that spelled *shady*. When you start looking for shady, you find it everywhere. A man, his sweat-stained cap pulled low over his eyes, drunkenly weaved from one lamppost to another on Second Street. Two young and unwashed ruffians filched green apples from a cart outside Henley's Grocery. A woman wearing too much lip rouge crabbed loudly at her husband as they stepped out of Greenwald's photographic studio on Main—a photographic studio with river photographs displayed in the storefront window. River panoramas, really. Charcoals and soft grays, the sleepy colors of the river in the last light at the end of the day. Flat, still images, but so real looking, so alive, it wouldn't have taken much imagination to see the frames as small windows on the river itself.

I don't know how long I stood there, my eyes moving from one photograph to another. Five minutes, perhaps, or fifteen, and I don't how long I might have remained lost in the seeing if not for a voice startling me back to there and then. "Tell me what you see," the voice said.

I spun around to find myself face to face with, as he would later introduce himself, Mr. George Greenwald, the photographer. "I . . . I see the river, sir."

"I've been studying you studying the photographs, and I saw something in your eyes, something lost on most people. I could be mistaken, though I don't think so. Look again and tell me what you really see."

I didn't need to look again. "I see quiet, sir."

Mr. Greenwald linked his fingers together and shook hands with himself. "Exactly! You have the gift. It's rare, you know, the ability to see beyond the surface of things. Rare indeed." He stepped back then, unclasped his hands, and held them in the air as if shaping a frame. Looking through this frame, turning his head this way and that, he appeared to be studying my face. "Has anyone ever told you that you have exquisitely beautiful eyes?"

Hardly. *Exquisite* wasn't a word people in my acquaintance bandied about, though I didn't say that. I didn't say anything, in fact, because I was too busy trying to think of a polite way to take my leave of Mr. Greenwald.

"Well, of course, they have. Here's a better question—have you ever been photographed?"

Only once, though I didn't say that either. A traveling photographer had come by our farm one summer, and Mama had given him a week's worth of egg money to take a picture of the family. Wanting us to look dignified, she'd insisted on our best posture and forbidden us to smile. We'd come out looking like a family waiting in line for the undertaker's parlor.

"I must be going now," I said.

"Not so quick. You must allow me to take your photograph."

"I'm sorry, sir, but I really must be going," I said, then turned and began walking my distrust briskly away.

"There'll be no charge," he called after me.

I kept walking and had made it nearly to the end of the block, nearly to the corner, nearly out of his sight, when he called, "I'll pay you a dollar."

I stopped as quickly and surely as if I'd collided with a stone wall. I turned. "How long will it take, sir?" I called back.

A smile broke out on Mr. Greenwald's face. "Not long, fifteen or twenty minutes."

"Might we do it here . . . here on the sidewalk?"

"Is that the only way you will agree?"

"Yes, sir. The only way."

The sidewalk was certainly safe, what with the crowd that soon gathered round to gawk. Unaccustomed to being the center of such attention, I distracted myself by watching Mr. Greenwald assemble his equipment. The leather-covered camera box was attached atop a three-legged wooden stand. The front of the box folded down and the camera workings slid forward like an accordion. In the center of these workings was a perfectly round glass eye. The photographic plates fitted into a door that folded down in the back. Simple, everyday materials—wood, leather, glass, metal—arranged in a brilliantly mysterious way. Oh, how I ached to see what the camera saw. I had to clasp my hands behind my back to quell a strong urge to touch.

When Mr. Greenwald had finished setting up, he turned to the crowd. "Light," he instructed, "is the key element in photography. It's light, reflecting off the subject, that is recorded on the photographic plate. And you are blocking the light, so please step back."

The crowd murmured, then stepped back. "Ready?" he asked.

I stiffened my spine, squared my shoulders, dignified my jaw, and nodded.

"No, no, no," Mr. Greenwald said, throwing his hands in the air. "I need for you to relax."

I relaxed, a little.

"More," he said, leaning forward and pressing his eye to the camera back.

I relaxed some more, or at least I thought I did.

Mr. Greenwald took his turn at spine-straightening and jaw-tightening. He stood like that for a moment, his hands on his hips. Then, an idea sparked in his eyes, and he dashed inside the shop and removed one of the river panoramas from the window. Upon returning to the sidewalk, Mr. Greenwald pulled a boy out of the crowd and asked him to hold the photograph to the right of the camera.

"Look into this, block out everything except the quiet, like before."

I looked. I blocked. I lost myself in the seeing, and the next thing I knew, Mr. Greenwald was pressing a dollar bill into my hand. "Stop in tomorrow morning. By then I'll have you developed and displayed in the window."

"The window?"

"Best advertisement there is. Every woman in town will want me to take her photograph in hopes that I'll be able to make her look as beautiful as you."

I shivered at the thought of this—strangers standing and staring at me long after I'd left Muscatine, perhaps even after I'd returned to Nebraska at the end of the summer, perhaps I'd still be there, gathering dust, the same time next year. Me and the evil-eyed men in the WANTED posters. Had I, as Mama might have said, sold my soul for a dollar?

Mr. Greenwald's photographic studio put an end to my shady-search of Muscatine, though I kept an eye out for the wolf whistlers as I hurried back along the path. To my way of thinking, wolf whistlers and bank robbers were kissing cousins. Their camp was quiet.

I didn't tell Hannah about Mr. Greenwald and the photograph when I returned to the *Oh My*. I might have, if a fresh wolf-whistle hadn't rung out just as I was about to ascend the boarding plank. I craned my head around, and there was one of those clammer fellows, coming out of the shady woods, an ax balanced on his shoulder. Murder fresh on my mind, I bent down and grabbed up the only weapon readily available, a fistful of sand. And then the other clammer fellow stepped out of the shady woods. He was pushing Hannah's wheelbarrow, stacked high with fresh-cut wood. Balanced on top of the load was the splitting maul. And balanced atop his shoulder was a . . . a wolf-whistling parrot!

"Sorry, miss. Paddy's first owner taught him to whistle like that. I've been trying to unteach him, but I'm not having much luck."

Paddy then cut loose with three wolf whistles in a row.

"At least he has good taste," the ax-wielding clammer said, grinning.

The sand sifted down from my hand.

As it turned out, Hannah had made a trade with the clammers— restocking our firewood for a home-cooked meal and, as an unspoken bonus, an evening's worth of male conversation for Isaac. And it was a fascinating conversation, at least the part I overheard while clearing away the supper dishes. The clammer fellows, Al Rigler and John Treakwell, after washing the work from their hands and faces, weren't shady at all. In the winter months, they taught at the high school in Iowa City. Albert taught mathematics and John, Paddy's owner, taught science. Both were bachelors, and supplemented their "paltry" teacher incomes by clamming in the summer months. The clams they harvested weren't really clams. They were mussels. The going rate for mussel shells at the button factories in Muscatine was twelve dollars a ton. The real prize, if a clammer was lucky enough to find one, was freshwater pearls. In the thousands and thousands of mussel shells they'd steamed and opened the previous summer, they'd found only one with a pearl in its belly. They'd sold the pearl to a buyer for seventy dollars.

If I had been a dog, my ears would have perked up and my tail wagged. Little had I known that money, wheelbarrows heaped high with it, could be plucked from the river mud.

The conversation was just getting around to clamming boats, metal hooks, and cooking boxes when Hannah pulled me aside. "There's a couple of hours of daylight left, and I was thinking this would be a good time for your first swimming lesson," she whispered.

If I had been Paddy the parrot and my owner had taught me to curse, that would have been the time. Instead, I whispered, "Sure."

After walking a short distance north along the shore, we came to a back channel that was separated from the main channel by a sliver of an island. "This'll do just fine," Hannah said, then sat down on the bank and began unlacing her shoes.

"It's been a long day. Maybe it would be best to do this another time," I said, overcome by the memory of being trapped underwater.

"I understand your hesitation, Megan, truly I do, but learning to swim could save your life."

What she didn't say, though surely thought, was that if I'd known how to swim, Isaac wouldn't have reinjured his leg diving in to save me from drowning. Guilt got me out of my shoes and stockings.

Hannah bared more than her feet. Leaving her shirt and trousers folded neatly on the shore, she waded into the water wearing only her camisole and bloomers.

"What if someone happens by?" I asked.

"Duck," Hannah answered, then did.

I unbuttoned.

I waded in . . . ankle deep, shin deep, knee deep. Waist deep! Something slithery brushed my leg. Trying to run in water, I soon learned, was like trying to run with boat anchors for shoes.

Hannah was beside me then. "Close your eyes, fill your lungs with air, and then immerse yourself and stay under for as long as you can hold your breath."

I gulped air. I bent my knees, and a gurgling rush swallowed me. I might have panicked if I hadn't forgotten the part about closing my eyes. My hand, turned this way and that in front of my face, seemed to glow in its greenish whiteness. My bloomers billowed. Bubbles burst from my nostrils. I was so fascinated with this new way of seeing that I was almost perturbed when Hannah pulled me to the surface, though my lungs were awfully glad.

Seeing made the swimming lessons easy. Floating on my back wasn't that different from lying in prairie grass. And floating on my stomach, eyes wide and watchful, was like pulling back the curtain on a new, though blurry, world. If flying means you move your arms back and forth and your feet are no longer touching the face of the earth, then treading water was as close to flying as I suspect a body can get.

Though it would take more practice for me to get good at co-ordinating my arms and legs to propel myself across the surface of the water, Hannah declared me a "fish" and handed me a hunk of her homemade soap, which she'd used to bathe herself with while I'd learned to float.

Thankfully, Al and John, along with the wolf whistler, had returned to their camp before Hannah and I, wearing only our outer clothing and carrying the wet wads of our underthings, returned from our swim.

"How did it go?" Isaac asked.

I crossed my arms over my chest. "I swam."

"And?"

"And I didn't drown."

"And?"

Isaac wasn't giving up. "And I loved it," I answered, then rambled on and on about seeing underwater. There was something else I was thinking, though didn't say—I was already dreading going home at the end of summer because there weren't any rivers near our farm, and even if there were, Mama would never allow me to go swimming, even fully dressed.

I swam through my dreams that night. The bottom of my dream river was littered with greedy mussels. Some had dollar bills hanging like green tongues from the seams of their crescent-shaped jaws. Try as I might, I couldn't tug even one of those bills free. Other mussels, their outer shells encrusted with pearls, turned to globs of mud at a finger's touch. One mussel changed its shape into that of a photographic camera, pointed itself at me, then sprouted a tailfin and fled into the shadows. I swam after it, using long, graceful strokes, and soon found myself on an underwater street, my reflection wavy in the storefront window glass. And then I came upon Mr. Greenwald's photography studio. Mama was there in the window. She was flat as a flapjack and colored in shades of gray, as if carefully scissored from a life-size photograph. Her brow was pleated, and her eyes were set for scolding. Her mouth was set for scolding, too, though only a gush of bubbles came out when she tried to speak.

Thinking I'd try to convince Mama that her rules sank like

rocks when it came to the river, I opened my own mouth. You need air to make words, and my lungs, content until that moment, screamed their emptiness. I waved goodbye to Mama, who was tapping her foot impatiently, and then clawed my way upward through the water, only to bang my head again and again on a solid sky.

Evening Edition

July 2, 1896

SIDEWALK STIR

MUSCATINE, IOWA—Megan Barnett, a visitor to our fair city, created quite a stir yesterday afternoon when she agreed to pose for a photograph on the street in front of Greenwald's photographic studio. The photograph is now on display in Mr. Greenwald's window, and he invites all the young women of Muscatine to come on down and admire his work.

Chapter 13

LEAVING MUSCATINE BEHIND

I WAS GLAD TO WAKE UP FROM THE DREAM, AND GLAD TO LEAVE MUS-catine and Mr. Greenwald's photograph of me behind as we steamed into the channel the next morning. Like the morning before, I joined Isaac in the boiler room. Unlike the morning before, Isaac chose to lie on the padded woodbin instead of sitting on the chair, and he chose to put me in charge. With Isaac looking on, I pumped the water, fed the fire, read the gauges, answered Hannah's bells with a right or left twist of a valve.

Sometime along about midmorning, Isaac fell asleep. Hard asleep, and when I realized this, the boiler room felt an entirely different place. I'd only seen pictures of a jungle, though that was exactly what came to mind. The piston's beat—a native's drum. The tangle of pipes—a hissing den of snakes. The boiler itself—a cannibal's steaming supper cauldron. My shirt was soaked through with perspiration, and I might have drowned in my fear if not for the windows on either side. They brought a breeze, and more importantly, they framed scenes of calm. Channel markers bobbed rhythmically, white herons waded in the shallow marshes, and everyday life played out along the shores. A woman pegged her wash to a line, a barefoot boy dangled his fishing line from a wooden dock, and a log raft, floating a genuine, white-steepled church, drifted by. Men steered with poles at each of the raft's four corners, and I had to smile when I imagined a whole congregation holding tight to the edge of the pews and praying hard for a safe delivery to wherever on earth they were going. I did some praying for safe deliveries myself.

Jon-Jacob answered my prayers. He burst into the boiler room, shouting, "Papa, Papa. Did you see the church?" Isaac didn't wake, so Jon-Jacob shook his shoulder. Isaac still didn't wake, and Jon-Jacob turned his puzzled look to me.

"Papa won't wake up."

I stepped away from the boiler and touched Isaac's forehead. "Quick, run and get your mama."

Hannah was there in a blink, bending over Isaac and saying, "Megan, take over for me in the wheelhouse. I've locked the wheel with a leather strap. Remove the strap and don't worry about anything except keeping her in the channel; the chart shows submerged boulders up ahead."

I backed away—from Hannah, from her words and their meaning. I backed right into the pantry, then into the living quarters. If I hadn't backed into the table, I might have backed myself all the way home. The table woke me up, and got me turned around and moving up the wheelhouse ladder.

The wheel, after I removed the holding strap and wrapped my hands about it, felt twice its former size. I breathed deep, hoping to steady my thoughts and especially my good-at-seeing eyes. To their horror, a tow and barge bore down hard and fast from the north, a small fishing boat lay ahead, and the river, in the spaces not taken up by boats I was likely going to crash the *Oh My* into, shone with ripples of every sort.

What I wanted to do was just stop—right there in the middle of the river, the way you stop a horse with a tug of the reins and a *Whoa!* But the river wasn't solid like the farm. You couldn't just stop, like a bird can't just decide to stop flapping its wings in midair. I'd have to do something, and I'd have to do it quick.

The barge, with its size and speed, presented the largest threat, no question there. Remembering Hannah's direction that less is better than more when it comes to steering, I eased the wheel to the right. The *Oh My* answered with a slight—too slight—turn to the left, so I eased some more, and some more, and some more until I was quite sure I'd less-is-mored us away from the barge . . . and into a direct line with the fishing boat! Oars in the water and rowing, the fisher fellow didn't see us coming because he was facing upstream. The channel narrowed ahead, leaving me no room to pass the fishing boat either on the right or left, and the gap between us was closing fast. I reached for the *Oh My*'s whistle cord. I gritted my teeth. I yanked.

WHORAROARAROAR. WHORAROARAROAR.

The fellow in the fishing boat stood bolt upright as if attached to puppet strings. His boat teetered. He teetered, and I was sure he was one teeter away from going overboard when, just in the nick of time, he sat back down, took up his oars, and began rowing fast— not toward the shallows, as I'd expected, but toward the center of the channel. Either he was dumber than I was about the river, or in such a panic that his good sense had abandoned ship.

Jon-Jacob flew up the ladder just then. "Mama says I should tell you she's going to slow us down, and . . . and . . . there was something else. Oh yeah, I remember. Mama says you're doing fine." And then Jon-Jacob flew down the ladder again, and I was alone again and definitely not fine. Beads of perspiration—or maybe even tears—stung my eyes.

I wiped at my eyes and, in doing so, cleared the way for a flicker of hope. The fisher fellow, smartly stopping short of bashing into the barge, had turned the nose of his little boat upstream again. If he stayed put, and I steered the *Oh My* to the far right, I might yet miss him. I gave the wheel a healthy turn. The *Oh My* answered by veering sharply right, taking aim on a channel buoy. I straightened us out and sized up the situation. Yes, I thought, if the fisher fellow kept on his path, there was just enough room to squeeze between his boat and the buoy.

And it might have worked if not for the barge beginning its pass of the fishing boat about then. Furrowing the water like a plow furrows earth, the barge pushed up waves that were like hands, shoving the fishing boat right back into my path, and closing fast. Easing wouldn't do. A healthy turn wouldn't do. I spun the wheel—just as the barge's wake slapped the *Oh My.* I closed my eyes and braced myself. In the first second, I thought about how captains always went down with their ship. In the next second, I decided I wasn't truly the captain. And in the next I heard Mama's voice saying, "I told you fourteen was too young for a girl to travel alone."

Several more seconds passed, with no shuddering jolt and no sound of scraping or splintering wood. I chanced opening my eyes. The river ahead was blessedly clear. I'd missed the fisher fellow. I'd missed the buoy. I wasn't going to die. No one was going to die. Relief filled me like hot chocolate on a bitterly cold winter night.

My relief chilled soon enough, though. Eyes wide then, I saw that I'd spun the *Oh My* right out of the channel. And my relief turned to ice when I saw the telltale ripples of some submerged thing, dead ahead. I eased left, and was about to ease left again when Hannah's hand fell on my shoulder. I nearly jumped out of my skin.

"You are amazing, simply amazing," she said.

I didn't feel amazing, though I did feel glad. Glad that Hannah was about to relieve me. I went to step aside for Hannah, but she stepped back.

"I need you to stay at the wheel," she said. "The fisherman is in the water and we need to pull him out."

"Did I hit him?"

"No. He got caught between the barge's wake and ours, and his boat capsized. Take her back into the channel, straighten the rudder, and then I'll stop the engine and we'll let her drift backward with the current. When we come alongside the buoy the poor fellow is clinging to, I'll throw him a rope. Once he's onboard, pick a likely spot, you know by now what I look for, and steer for shore. I'll do everything else."

"Maybe I should go below, work the engine, and you should steer."

"You'll do fine. No. Better than fine. Just go with your instincts, the way you did back there. I'll run the engine and tend to Isaac."

"Is Isaac awake?"

The cheery mask that Hannah had put on her face peeled away. "On and off. His fever is awfully high."

"Go. I'll manage here," I said.

Chapter 14

ROCK ISLAND

IT ALL HAPPENED AS HANNAH HAD SAID IT WOULD. ONCE I'D GOTTEN US back into the channel, narrowly missing both the ripples and a second buoy, the paddlewheel stopped slapping the water. The *Oh My* paused, then, caught by the current, began drifting backward. Hannah threw the fisher fellow a rope, reeled him in, started the engine again, and I began looking for a likely place to land.

I set my sights on the very next island. A boat, twice the size of the *Oh My*, was tied there and, more importantly, I needed to find all of us a solid perch. Sounds of someone on the ladder. I turned to look down and saw the top of a balding head rising up. The fisher fellow, come to chastise me for my lousy piloting. I stiffened my back. The man, once fully in the wheelhouse, came to stand beside me. He was tall and of a beefy build. Gray hairs peppered his beard. I returned my gaze to the river, though I could feel his eyes were still on me, could feel his wet clothes cooling the space between us. *Why doesn't he say something?* I thought. And that thought led to a new thought. *Why hadn't Hannah come along to make a formal introduction?* And then—*What if he's one of the fellows from the WANTED posters! What if he has already harmed Hannah, Isaac, and Jon-Jacob and is about to make a clean sweep of it by harming me!* I shot him a mean glance and blurted, "I'm stronger than I look."

Fisher fellow's eyes opened wide, as if thunderstruck, and then he smiled. "How old are you?"

"Older than I look."

He thrust a hand at me then, and I batted it away. He pulled back. "I mean no harm. Truly I don't. It's just that Mrs. Bradshaw told me her sister was piloting, and I imagined you to be much older, a matronly, time-hardened type. And here you are, so young and lovely. You rendered me speechless, and that doesn't happen very often. May we start over? I'm Matthew Miller. Dr. Matthew Miller, but you must call me Doc."

And then it was me who was thunderstruck. According to Mama, doctors were second only to God, and I'd just batted this doctor's hand, which he offered again. I shook it.

"How long have you been piloting?" he asked.

"About an hour, sir."

"I don't mean how long have you been at the wheel today, I mean how long altogether?"

"About an hour, sir."

"That's not possible. Only an expert pilot could have performed the maneuvers you performed back there."

"I'm telling the truth, sir."

"Well, I'll be. Any other pilot would have mowed me down, especially after I panicked and rowed into the channel instead of out. You may just have saved my life."

Doc's comment must have muddled my mind because the next thing out of my mouth wasn't very heroic. "Hannah wants me to put us ashore soon, sir. And I don't mean to be rude, but I need you to be quiet so I can concentrate."

"No need. I had two reasons for coming up here. First, to thank you, and second to tell you that Mrs. Bradshaw has agreed that we'll take her on upriver and tie her to the dock of my summer house near the mouth of the Rock River. I can't properly treat your brother-in-law's infection without the medicines I keep in my office."

Medicines for Isaac! "How far?"

"About a mile."

I drew in a mile-long breath and began scanning the river ahead for traffic, snags, ripples, and doctors disguised as fisher fellows in small wooden boats.

"I can take the wheel, if you like. I've done a little piloting in my time."

This from a fellow who had rowed the wrong way in a panic. "I'm fine," I said, "though I wouldn't mind a second set of eyes."

"Speaking of eyes, has anyone ever told you that yours are absolutely enchanting?"

I lifted my right index finger from the wheel.

"Let me be the second then, and tell me, have you ever been photographed?"

That was safer ground. I nodded, then said, "I'd much rather have been the one behind the lens, taking the photograph, than the one posing in front of it."

"Ah, a budding photographer."

"Hardly."

"Well, you just never know."

Jon-Jacob joined us soon after, and kept Doc occupied with questions. Could he fix his papa's leg? Had he caught any fish? Was he going to come back and try to find his boat? Did he like snakes? Had he ever eaten fried oatmeal? Were there any boys at his house?

I eavesdropped on Doc's answers. He couldn't promise, but he'd do his best to fix Isaac's leg. Yes, he had caught several prize-size fish, though they'd gone down with his boat, which, regrettably, he'd have to leave at the bottom of the river. He thought snakes were admirable. He'd not eaten fried oatmeal, and there were no boys at his house, only a very lonely Shetland pony he kept for when his nieces came for a visit.

* * *

Doc's summer home was a bit south of the Rock Island levee, which, as I could see from a distance, was clogged with boats. This was a relief, as I'd never been good at threading needles. Doc talked me through the necessary turn that took us into a corset-tight squeeze of a back channel. "Are you sure the *Oh My* will fit, sure it won't scrape bottom?" I asked. Doc assured me that boats larger than the *Oh My* sometimes used the channel as a shortcut between the Rock and Mississippi Rivers. Hannah worked her magic on the engine, slowing us at the right time, cutting power at the right time. When we were within a few yards of the dock, Doc raced down the ladder and tied us off. I stepped away from the wheel—feeling relief, exhaustion, and a whole lot of pride.

Doc was all business once we were connected to solid land. A footpath led away from the dock, and he wasted no time sprinting up this path and disappearing into the woods.

I joined Hannah, Isaac, and Jon-Jacob in the boiler room. Isaac was awake. He was still quite pale, but managed to move a hand to his forehead in a shaky salute. I couldn't help but grin as I saluted him back.

Before Doc returned, Hannah had changed the linens on their bed, and I'd started a fire in the cookstove and filled a kettle with water from the rain barrel. The water hadn't yet begun to boil when the good doctor rushed in, toting his black bag and a very thick, leather-clad medical book. He set these down on the table and then hefted Isaac from the woodbin bed and carried him to the freshly made bed in the cabin.

Turning to Jon-Jacob, Doc said, "At the end of the path, you'll find a corral. Would you mind keeping my lonely pony company while I'm fixing up your father's leg?"

Jon-Jacob turned to Hannah, hope replacing the sadness in his eyes.

"If you promise not to go any farther than the corral."

"I promise," Jon-Jacob answered.

Once Jon-Jacob was out of the room, Doc bent over Isaac's leg and began to cut away the bandages. I had to fight not to gag when the infection's foul odor overpowered the air in the room. Hannah didn't flinch. She gathered up the soiled bandages, tossed them into the cookstove fire, and then returned to Isaac's bedside.

After examining Isaac's wound and then taking the time to pore over several pages in the thick book, Doc said, "This doesn't look good."

Isaac, as if startled full awake by Doc's pronouncement, lifted his head. "Doc in Keokuck wanted to amputate, but I wasn't having it, and I'm not having it now. Got to have two good legs to take care of my family."

"Butchers," Doc spat.

Isaac let his head fall back onto the pillow. "You got any magic tricks there in your black bag that'll fix me up?" Isaac asked.

"No magic, but I have powders that might bring down your fever. And Doc . . . uh . . . there I've gone and done it again, referred to myself in the third person. Comes from talking to my youngest patients. They like that, when I say 'Doc would like you to stick out your tongue now.' Anyway, I've had some luck slowing an infection by spraying wounds with a mixture of water and carbolic acid. Trouble is, there's already signs of gangrene. That's the odor you smell. The dead flesh needs to be removed, but if I try to remove it surgically, I'd likely have to cut away too much healthy flesh or damage the blood supply and the wound might never heal together properly."

"Is there another way?" Hannah asked, and Doc bent over his book again. When he'd rifled through a dozen or so pages without a word, an idea that had been worming its way through my mind wiggled out. "What about maggots?"

"Maggots?" Isaac asked with a visible shiver.

"Or was it leeches? I don't know . . . seems I remember reading about one or the other in a . . . somewhere." I stopped short of saying that I'd read about maggots or leeches in one of Jake's dime novels. Mama had forbidden me to read them, saying they could cause a girl nervous problems, so I'd read them on the sly in the hayloft. They'd taken me places I thought I'd never get to go—like deepest, darkest Africa and the Amazon jungle. And the only nervousness I'd suffered was in worrying that Mama might find me out.

Doc closed the medical book. "I seem to recall hearing the same thing Megan has heard, about introducing maggots to a badly infected wound."

"Could it do any harm?" Hannah asked.

Doc rubbed his temple, then said, "Harm? No, I don't suppose."

"Maggots it is then," Isaac said.

"Allow me to try other remedies first. I'll give you a powder that will bring down your fever and another that will make you drowsy, and then I'll clean out the wound with soap and water, finishing off with carbolic acid."

"Yes, of course," Hannah agreed.

And then Doc rolled up his sleeves and went to work. He withdrew two vials from within his black bag and added three shakes of white powder from each vial to a spoonful of water, then held the spoon to Isaac's lips. Isaac took his medicine, then scrunched his face and swallowed hard.

While Doc waited for Isaac to become groggy, he scrubbed his hands with hot water and lye soap. As he scrubbed, he told us that recent scientific discoveries had convinced him and many of his colleagues of the importance of sterilizing both their instruments and hands before working on patients. "Bacteria can't be seen with the naked eye, but they're everywhere. Each of us has colonies of the little creatures living on our unwashed hands."

I'd studied my own hands many times, the walnut-shell shape of the knuckles, the rising moons of the nails, and the hills and valleys of the palms. I studied them again, front and back, and then asked, "Can bacteria be found in river water?"

"Any water that's stagnant, like that along the shore."

"Could bacteria be the cause of Isaac's infection?"

"Could be."

I turned and walked straight into the pantry, where I snatched up a pair of Hannah's trousers. Off came my skirt. Off came my petticoat. One leg in, and then the other. When I pulled up the trousers, my bloomers bunched. I reached down each leg to smooth out the bloomers and then buttoned the fly before returning to Isaac's bedside.

Doc spent quite a lot of time cleaning out Isaac's wound. When he had finished, he consulted the medical book one more time before suggesting that Hannah and I step outside. "Carbolic acid works well as a disinfectant, but when it's released into the air, it can cause a burning sensation in your eyes."

At some point while Hannah and I were waiting outside on the deck, she noticed that I was wearing trousers. She looked at me with a question in her eyes.

"I'm done wearing skirts, at least when I'm onboard the *Oh My*. Isaac told me that skirts and riverboats don't mix. That likely my skirts were responsible for my getting tangled and trapped beneath the boat. If I'd been wearing trousers, he wouldn't have had to rescue me. If I'd been wearing trousers, then his leg wouldn't be crawling with bacteria and he'd be healed by now."

"You're not responsible in any way."

"Maybe not. But I figure it's safer for everyone if I wear trousers like you do."

"And I think they look rather fetching," Doc said, stepping outside. I'm sure I blushed.

"How's Isaac?" Hannah asked.

"He's resting now," Doc answered, rubbing his eyes as if they were smarting. "Let him sleep as long as he can, and I'll come back in a few hours to check on him."

"About the maggots. Do you have any advice?" Hannah asked.

"I'll search through back issues of my medical journals, see what I can find. Meantime, someone might want to go out and round up a handful of the little critters."

"I'll go," I said to Hannah.

"Are you sure?"

"I'm sure."

Chapter 15

MAGGOT HUNTING

I WALKED UP THE PATH AND INTO THE WOODS WITH DOC, AND A LITTLE ways along we came to a clearing and a small stucco and wood-beamed cottage that put me in mind of Hansel and Gretel. Doc excused himself and entered the cottage through the front door, which was curved at the top instead of squared off. I wondered then what kind and shape of door Horace was making at that very moment. One thing I knew. Whatever the shape, Horace's doors would be easy to open and easy on the eye.

Jon-Jacob was perched on the top rail of the corral fence, petting the pony's nose. "Is Papa okay?" he asked when I draped an arm across his shoulder.

"He's sleeping."

"Whew. I was just telling the pony how worried I was. Do you think Mama will mind if I stay a little longer? This pony is awful lonely."

"I don't think she'll mind."

I left Jon-Jacob and headed farther into the woods, glad for the freedom the trousers gave me—no worry of my skirts catching on a bramble; no worry about tripping while stepping over a log. It wasn't long before my nose picked up a likely scent, and in a few more paces, I spied the prize. At their best, skunks smell pretty bad. After two or three days dead, they're putrid. The foul odor didn't seem to bother the two beady-eyed crows who had already claimed the skunk for their own. "Sorry, fellows," I said as I approached. The crows looked at me as if to say, "But we found it first." I waved my arms in the air. "Shoo!" The crows spread their wings and flew close over my head, causing me to duck. After landing in a nearby tree, they scolded me with loud caws.

I clasped my nose between a finger and thumb and then squatted beside the dead skunk. The mama flies had done their job. The carcass was bloated with hundreds of maggots about the size, color, and shape of cooked rice.

I didn't have the stomach to carry the dead skunk and its stink all the way back to the *Oh My*, so I unclasped my nose and did something that would have caused Mama to have a heart attack. I began plucking maggots from the skunk's innards with the fingers of my right hand and depositing them into the palm of my left. "Rice. It's only rice," I repeated to myself. It was hard to convince myself, though. Rice doesn't wiggle, and the rice pot doesn't stink to high heaven.

When I'd retrieved about a dozen, I closed my fingers over my little captives, stood, and, as I ran past the waiting crows, I called, "He's all yours now, and you're welcome to him."

Back on the *Oh My*, after dropping the maggots into an empty baking soda tin that Hannah quickly fetched for me, I scrubbed my hands until they were raw. Ten minutes later, I scrubbed them again. It was the stubborn wiggle that I couldn't seem to wash away.

Isaac was still sleeping. "Has he stirred?" I asked.

"No, not yet. His fever does seem to have come down and his breathing is steady, so I think sleep is a blessing for him right now," Hannah answered.

"What do you suppose was in those powders Doc gave him?"

"I have no idea, though whatever it was, it must have been powerful." Hannah pulled a chair away from the table and sat down.

I did the same. "What do you suppose Mama would say if she could see us now?" I asked, pointing to the men's trousers we both wore.

Hannah grinned. "She'd probably take to her bed for a while. Then, after the initial shock wore off, I think she'd be proud, especially of you. You're a wonder, Megan. Steering us out of harm's way, magically scaring up a doctor, coming up with the maggots. Isaac and I would be in an even bigger fix if not for you."

I was about to tell Hannah that her praise would be better served if she lavished it on herself, when Jon-Jacob burst into the cabin. He made a beeline for Isaac's bed. Before Hannah could stop him, he grabbed Isaac's shoulder and tried to shake him awake. Isaac didn't stir. Jon-Jacob turned to us then, with tears in his eyes. His bottom lip quivered. "Is Papa dead?"

Hannah rushed to Jon-Jacob and scooped him up. "He's only sleeping."

"Are you sure?"

"I'm absolutely, positively, undeniably, one hundred percent sure."

"When will he wake up? I want to tell him about the pony."

"I have an idea," Hannah said. "Why don't you pull a chair up to your Papa's bed, hold his hand, and tell him all about the pony. Your voice might work its way into his dreams, and he'll feel better just knowing you're walking beside him. Meantime, Auntie Megan and I will whip up something to eat. I'll bet you're hungry."

"Starved," Jon-Jacob said, dragging one of the chairs to the edge of Isaac's bed.

Hannah turned to me. "Is there something you're particularly hungry for?"

"Anything, as long as it doesn't have rice in the recipe," I answered.

"Don't I remember that you used to love rice pudding, couldn't get enough of it?"

"That was before I got acquainted with maggots."

"Oh."

I don't know if it was the steam from Hannah's split pea soup or the aroma of my corn bread that roused Isaac from his powder sleep. Upon opening his eyes, Jon-Jacob asked, "Was I in your dream, Papa?"

Isaac's eyes fell closed again, and I was afraid that he'd fallen back asleep, but then he opened them again and whispered, "Pony."

"That's it, Papa, I was telling you about Doc's pony."

"Doc?"

Hannah stepped in. "I'll tell you all about it after you have a few sips of this tea I've been keeping warm for you."

Hannah lifted Isaac's head with one hand and held the cup to his lips with the other. Isaac took small, slow sips.

"How long have I been asleep?" he asked when he'd had enough and pushed the cup away.

"Exactly the right amount of time," Hannah answered, then pecked a kiss on his forehead.

Doc returned to the *Oh My* soon after Isaac awoke. "I remember now," Isaac said when Doc approached his bed. Isaac patted his covers for his legs. Finding them still attached, he fell back against his pillow and sighed.

"Don't worry, son. I wouldn't amputate without your knowledge. Besides, I've found some hopeful articles in my medical journals. One regarding maggots and another regarding leeches. Maggots dine on the infection and leeches increase the blood flow to the area around the wound."

I fetched the baking soda tin and handed it over to Doc. He peered inside and pretended a shiver. "I've known a lot of young women in my life, but not one of them would have been brave enough to touch these disgusting little critters."

He'd meant this as a compliment, I was almost sure, though I felt like I needed to explain. "I tricked my eyes into seeing grains of cooked rice."

He smiled. "And what trick would you play on your eyes for leeches?"

"I've only read about them in a book, so I'd have to see a real one before I could decide. I'll go look for some, if only you'll tell me where I might find them."

Hannah stepped forward. "You've had more than your share of unpleasantness for one day. It's my place."

"Are you sure?" I asked.

"As sure as you were about maggot hunting," Hannah answered.

"Does this mean we're going swimming?" Jon-Jacob asked.

"Swimming it is."

Swimming. Seeing underwater. Floating. Flying. My whole body ached to go along, but someone would need to stay with Isaac, and it would have to be me. Or so I thought.

"You all go on. I'll stay here and keep Isaac company," Doc

offered, winking. It was the kind of wink that meant what it meant, so I followed Hannah and Jon-Jacob. We had only to go as far as the end of the dock, which Doc had said was a leech's favorite haunt.

Hannah removed her shoes and rolled her trousers up to her knees before climbing down a wobbly wooden ladder that was nailed to the end of the dock. Jon-Jacob stripped down to his drawers and, once Hannah gave him the go-ahead, he leapt into the water and began paddling about with such assuredness that one would have thought he had been born with fins. Like Hannah, I removed only my shoes. It wouldn't have done to remove more, what with Isaac and Doc being so close by.

I hadn't noticed how hot the afternoon air had become until I'd climbed down the ladder and slid into the cool water. It was like going from June to October. Swimming in trousers and shirt wasn't as pleasurable as swimming in only my underwear, though nearly so.

Jon-Jacob settled himself into a frantic routine. He'd climb the ladder and then take a flying leap. Arms holding his knees to his chest, he cannonballed into the water, raising an enormous splash. Each of his splashes sprayed a different shape. One resembled a rooster tail; another a sky-burst of Fourth of July fireworks.

Hannah stood motionless in the waist-deep water near a leg of the dock.

While Jon-Jacob plopped and Hannah stood, I practiced. Floating on my stomach, I delighted in seeing underwater, at least for as long as I could hold my breath. Floating on my back, I admired the ever-changing shapes in the clouds drifting lazily overhead—a napping dog, a two-headed squirrel, Horace's horseless carriage! It seemed like weeks since Horace had tumbled into my seat on the Eastbound, though it had only been a few days. Horace, who had called me "delightful." I wondered what kind of an evening he might be having in Plattsmouth—strolling through the city streets, perhaps, gazing into window fronts, tipping his cap to young women he passed. Pretty young women. Delightful young women. I rolled over and began practicing my crawl.

My arms quickly grew tired, so I set my feet down on the river bottom. One foot found mud; the other arched over something curved, hard, and quite rough. Thinking I might know what my foot had found, I reached down and brought up a palm-size mussel, like those I'd seen on the path back in Muscatine. It was too big to fit into my trouser pockets, so I tucked it under my chin as I two-handed my way up the ladder. I dripped a puddle as I stood there admiring my find. If the mussel held a pearl in its tightly clamped jaw, I'd have the money for my ticket home! Breaking into my treasure would have to wait, however.

Hannah had followed me up the ladder, and I soon saw that she'd been successful. Three slimy leeches had attached themselves to her ankles. I lay the mussel on one of the dock posts and asked, "Would you like me to pull them off?"

"Dabbing them with salt works better than pulling," she answered. "Jon-Jacob, would you fetch the salt shaker?"

Jon-Jacob left a watery footprint trail into the cabin. Doc followed him out, and as we waited for the leeches to fall free, he asked, "So, Megan. Now that you've seen a real leech, what trick of the eye would you use to describe them?"

I scrunched my nose. "Slivers of raw beef liver."

"Yum," Jon-Jacob said, rubbing his bare belly. "I love liver."

"Good for you," Doc said. "I've read that liver builds strong blood."

Jon-Jacob flexed his arms, showing his muscles.

Using a tweezers retrieved from his medical bag, Doc deposited six of the maggots and the three leeches at the edges of Isaac's wound.

"What if the leeches and maggots start fussing with each other?" Isaac asked as Doc wrapped his leg with a thin, though breathable, layer of gauze.

"I think they'll be too busy to notice."

All that night, a parade of thunderous storms battered the *Oh My*. Thunder on the prairie says what it has to say, then quickly goes away. Thunder on the river pulls up a chair and sits a spell, echoing off the bluffs, rumbling up the valleys. As I lay there, wide-eyed, the *Oh My* lashing about in the ferocious winds, I thought a lot about worrying. I was plenty worried about the storms, but mostly what I thought about was the idea of worrying itself. When Mama was worried, it was serious business. She'd put on a dour face and pucker her brow, and she expected the same from everyone in the house. For Mama, worrying was like praying—the more people who joined in, the quicker the problems would get solved. The trouble was that on the farm, there was always something to worry about—too much rain, not enough rain, a horse gone lame. Mama's brow was permanently puckered.

Hannah had a mess of things to worry about, but she rarely let it show. Hannah's way of worrying was easier on those around her, though holding it in was beginning to take its toll. Dark circles ringed her tired eyes, and she did little more than pick at her food. *Which way of worrying was best? Which was right? Which way was mine?*

Toward morning, I did fall asleep, though my dreams weren't so restful. In my dream river, the buoys were draped with dead skunks and the wheel wouldn't turn. Fishing boats bobbed to the left, the right, before me, and behind. Down below, a voice shouted, "Boiler's about to blow." Then, in a blink, I was on land and face-to-face with a masked man. He handed me a paper-wrapped bundle. I peeled away the wrapping to find a slab of ham, infested with maggots. Looking up again, the mask grinned an evil grin and then lunged as if to grab me. I tried to run but fell flat on my face because one of my legs was missing. I woke with a start and, as was my habit with dreams, I lay there in the dark, and tried to fit the dream pieces into the puzzle of the real. Everything fit except the masked man. I thought on that for a while, then fell into a dreamless sleep.

In the morning, when Hannah uncovered Isaac's wound, the leeches had nearly doubled in size. The wound didn't look much better, but it didn't look worse, either. "Time. It'll just take some time," Hannah said.

"Yep, by this time next week, I'll be dancing around the deck and clear off Doc's dock," Isaac added.

Isaac's mention of the dock reminded me of my mussel, which was nowhere to be found when I dashed out to retrieve it. Blown off the dock by the thunderstorm and carried away by the rain-swollen river, I guessed.

In the days we passed tied up at Doc's, Hannah and I weeded the rooftop garden, did the laundry, and scrubbed the *Oh My*'s decks until they shone. Work like I might have been doing for Mama back on the farm, but with a very big difference. On the farm, work was serious business. Mama didn't hold much with idle chatter, and stopping work before a chore was finished could bring out the willow whip as quickly and surely as could a sassy mouth. On the *Oh My*, Hannah and I talked as we worked. Talked about everything and about nothing, wherever the river of our conversation carried us. And our work was set aside to do things like admire a fossilized leaf in a rock Jon-Jacob had unearthed. Or respond to a called-out request from Isaac that we come look at a cartoon in an issue of *Harper's Magazine* that Doc had brought down for him to read. Or have a water fight with the leftover water in the scrubbing buckets. Amazingly, the work got done. It was like a math problem, and Hannah's equation worked as well as or better than Mama's.

Doc checked on Isaac's wound early each morning, and by the third day declared that genuine healing was taking place and that it would just be a matter of time before Isaac would be back on both feet again.

"Healed enough to travel?" Isaac asked with a grin.

"Not so quick," Doc answered. "I think it best if you wait a few more days, to build your strength."

Doc returned again each evening and brought along what he called his "piscatorial finery." Meaning fancy fishing gear. By Jon-Jacob's measure, Doc caught some beauties—walleye, black crappie, and one very ugly shovel-nosed sturgeon. By the fourth evening, Isaac hobbled out to the deck and joined Doc. Isaac tried his hand at casting a line from the whirring reel, but when the line tangled badly, he picked up his old bamboo pole and was content to sit there, watching his bobber while Doc reeled in his supper.

During the day, Doc saw patients at his office in town, though one day, when Jon-Jacob and I were feeding the pony a carrot from the rooftop garden, I could have sworn that I saw movement at one of the cottage windows. My good-at-seeing wasn't always trustworthy, though—I sometimes saw things that weren't really there at all. A stray strand of hair, hovering at the edge of my sight, was most often the cause. It had happened often enough, I'd wondered if that was how ghost stories got started, because of women with untidy hair.

Chapter 16

A PASSENGER

ON THE SIXTH MORNING, DOC ARRIVED JUST AS HANNAH AND I WERE preparing a breakfast of bacon and several days' worth of eggs that Jon-Jacob had gathered from the chicken coop on the *Oh My*'s roof. "Have you eaten?" Hannah asked.

"Feasted, in fact. Earned my way through medical school by working as a chef at one of those fancy Chicago hotels."

My curiosity got the best of me. "Did your mother teach you to cook?"

"Learned everything I needed to know from a book. But that's enough talk about me. How's the leg this morning?" he asked, pulling a chair up to Isaac's bedside.

"Leg's looking good, and I'm feeling so much stronger that Hannah and I have decided to leave in the morning."

"Your mind's made up then?" Doc asked.

"Yep. Mind's made up."

Doc began to unwind the gauze bandages and said, "I've been thinking that I could use a little vacation. My brother lives up in Winona, Minnesota, and he's been pestering me to come for a visit. Seeing as how you're heading upriver, I was wondering if you'd mind if I tagged along."

"You're welcome, of course," Hannah answered. "But what about your other patients?"

"I'll run a notice down to the newspaper office, and I'll post a note on my office door, referring my patients to one of the other doctors in town. That's the way it's done."

"How about the pony?" Jon-Jacob chimed in.

"There's a young fellow who lives down the road who would be more than happy to earn a couple of dollars feeding and watering the pony while I'm away."

Hannah looked as if she were ready to ask another question when Isaac interrupted. "Well, doesn't that beat all. We'll be traveling with our own private doctor."

By the time the sun pinked the next morning sky, Doc and his gear were aboard. He traveled light—medical bag and two medical books, a canvas duffle much like the one Horace had carried, his fancy fishing gear, and a wooden case with the words THE ECLIPSE NO. 3 printed in bold letters across the lid. Upon seeing the box, Jon-Jacob asked the question I was itching to ask. "What's that?"

"A photographic camera," Doc answered. "Figure I'll teach my-self how to use it while I'm onboard. Figure, if I ever get tired of doctoring, I might want to become a photographer. And I have Megan to thank for giving me the idea."

I don't know whose eyes were bigger, Jon-Jacob's or mine, though Jon-Jacob's second question, "Will you take my picture?" wasn't the question I would have asked. Not by a long shot. If I hadn't been biting my tongue, I'd have asked, "May I borrow it?"

Claiming to have quite a lot of experience with boilers and steam engines, Doc declared himself the boiler-room chief. Doc's promise of stories about the time he was a cowpoke out in Montana prompted Jon-Jacob to declare himself the boiler-room chief's first mate. Isaac would "supervise" from the padded woodbin, which, come night, would serve as the doctor's bed.

Hannah piloted us past the busy levees at Rock Island, Daven-port, and Moline and also through a treacherous section of river called the Rock Island Rapids. Even though, as Hannah explained, the Rapids had been tamed by the Army Corps of Engineers, which had blasted the boulders that had once littered the river bot-tom, pilots needed to be "at their keenest level of attention."

Once free of the rapids, Hannah turned the wheel over to me. "Are you ever not nervous at the wheel?" I asked.

"No," Hannah answered. "A little fear is a good thing. It keeps me on my toes."

Hannah and I took turns at the wheel that day—an hour on and an hour off. During one of Hannah's breaks, after promising to return in a blink if I hollered, she went below to check on the fellows. When she returned, she handed me a paper booklet. "Doc asked me to give you this. He says he can't make heads or tails of it and he's hoping you can help him out."

I read the title on the booklet's cover. *Operating Instructions: Eclipse No. 3.*

From that point on, I spent all my breaks buried in the instruction booklet. It was all very complicated. There were dry plates and exposures and chemicals. And when I wasn't on break, I scanned the river ahead for scenes that I thought might be worthy of being photographed. These scenes were everywhere. A bald eagle settling into a treetop nest; the undulating shadow of a railway bridge; a church steeple pointing up to God.

That evening, after we'd tied up at a pretty little island near Savanna, Illinois, Jon-Jacob swam and Hannah bared her ankles to blood-hungry leeches. I might have swum too, if not for the Eclipse No. 3. I'd read the booklet from front to back a dozen times and was still confused. "Best way to learn something new is to just roll up your sleeves and give it a try," Doc said. So we gave it a try.

Mostly Doc sat back and watched as I fumbled with the equipment, though once I had the camera securely affixed to the top of the tripod, he leapt before the lens and made silly faces while I bent and peered through the viewfinder. Something wasn't right. Where he stood on the shaded deck, his features were muted. I remembered then what Mr. Greenwald had said about light.

I was very careful carrying the camera and tripod down the boarding plank for fear the old troll would trip me up and the Eclipse No. 3 would fall into the water and drown.

Once onshore, I tried standing Doc in several positions—with the sun at his front, his back, and slanting in from the side. I chose the slant, as it looked to be the most flattering, and dropped the dry plate into the slot at the back of the Eclipse No. 3. The dry plate consisted of a frame, called the holder, a plate cover, and the plate itself, which was made of glass and coated with a sensitized gelatin. The cover protected the gelatin from premature exposure to light, but could be removed once inside the dark cave of the camera. "Ready?" I asked.

Doc mugged a smile.

Careful not to jiggle the camera, I removed the lens cap, which allowed light to flood the gelatin plate, counted to five, and then recapped the lens. Five seconds was the exposure time the instruction booklet recommended for taking a close-up photograph of a subject in natural light.

"Your turn," Doc said after I'd replaced the plate cover and removed the holder.

"Let's see if this one turns out before we waste a plate on me."

"We can always buy more."

Doc obviously hadn't grown up with a "waste not, want not" mama like mine. "We're losing our light, anyway. See there, the sun's about to sink behind the bluff."

"Tomorrow then. I'm not getting off this boat until I have a photograph of the beautiful young woman who saved my life."

A second sun rose and set inside my cheeks.

The pantry was the only room on the *Oh My* without windows, so it became our darkroom. We cleared the foodstuffs from a shelf to make room for the metal developing trays, and lit the wick in the small ruby lantern that had come with the kit. There were three bottles of chemicals in all. One was labeled TONER SOLUTION, and the other two were labeled DEVELOPING SOLUTION A and DEVELOP-ING SOLUTION B. *A* was for developing and *B* was for fixing.

I held the instruction booklet close to the eerie glow of the ruby lamp and read off the amount of each foul-smelling chemical that was required. Doc measured the amounts and I slipped the dry plate into the A-tray with the care and reverence of a minister per-forming a baptism.

And then we waited, and waited. When too much time had passed, I turned to Doc. "I think I must have done something wrong," I whispered, as if speaking in my normal voice would somehow spoil the developing process.

"Let's give it a little more time," Doc whispered back.

I soothed my eyes with a long blink, and when I opened them again, I thought I saw something. Faint, like a pattern in a wisp of smoke. Then, ever so slowly, a negative image began to appear. Doc wasn't Doc. He was light where he should have been dark, and dark where he should have been light. "It's magic," I said.

"No. It's not magic. It's me," he said, grinning in the reddened darkness.

"Do you think it's time we fixed you?"

"Fix away," he answered.

Using metal tongs that had come with the kit, I quickly removed the plate from the first tray and slid it into the second, which contained a solution that would stop, or fix, the image from continuing to develop.

The photograph wasn't a photograph until we had transferred the negative to a special "sensitive" paper, at which time Doc became Doc again—light where he should have been light, and dark where he should have been dark, and was, as he said, "a spitting good image."

We tidied up, returning the foodstuffs to the shelves and the Eclipse No. 3 paraphernalia to its case, before snuffing the ruby lamp and joining the others in the cabin. Hannah was the first to take a look. "Megan, this is very good. I think you may have found your calling."

Calling? Doctors were called to doctor. Preachers were called to preach. Hannah had been called to become a playwright. Horace had been called to build horseless carriages. *Was Hannah right? Was photography the thing I'd been born to do?* Maybe, if I had my own camera, though I couldn't see how that was going happen. There I was, with only one dollar and fifty cents and still without the faintest idea of how I would earn my way home.

Chapter 17

FOG

FOG. A HEAVY BLANKET OF THE STUFF KEPT US FROM GETTING AN EARLY start the next morning. Fog as dense and blinding as wind-driven snow. Fog like a close, gray box. We stayed put, but along about eight o'clock, we heard the distant though slow and methodic slap of a paddlewheel. The slap got louder, and then we could hear the chuffing of the engines. "Impatient fool," Isaac said, setting his coffee mug down on the table with a disgusted thud. Isaac's thud was answered with a thundering foghorn blast. Too close! Hannah caught Jon-Jacob's hand and said, "I think it's best if we all go ashore."

"I think you're right," Isaac said, reaching for his crutch.

I was the last down the boarding plank; Mama's carpetbag dangled from one hand, the Eclipse No. 3 case from the other.

We ran into the woods until we'd put several sturdy trees

between ourselves and the river. Isaac, standing on his good leg and using his crutch for support, cupped a hand to his mouth and shouted, "Ahoy there, you're about to go aground." We waited for an answer, and then we all joined Isaac's shout-then-listen choir. Doc with his booming bass. Isaac with his baritone. Hannah and I with our alto, and Jon-Jacob with his choirboy soprano. After the fourth pause, a voice shouted back. "Port or starboard?"

"Port!" Isaac hollered.

The fog began to swirl then, the way a lace curtain billows after a window is opened. And then the ghostly outline of the *Oh My* began to rock. "I can't bear to watch," Hannah said, turning away.

I couldn't bare *not* to watch. It was the least I could do for the *Oh My*, which was quaking in the waves sent out by the unseen boat.

The fog voice again. "Who are you?"

"The crew of the *Oh My*," Isaac answered.

It was on us then, the chuffing, the slapping, the bitter taste of the coal smoke, the droplets of her spray raining down on us like chill bumps.

"She's a long one," Isaac said, his voice thin as if talking through held breath.

"Seventy, eighty feet, from the time it's taking for her to pass," Doc added.

One last blast of the foghorn, the chuff and slap finally trailing off, the *Oh My* settling down, and the ghost boat was gone.

How does one get back to normal after a scare? A laugh works well, and Mama's carpetbag provided it. "Must have something pretty important hidden in there," Doc said as I carried it back onboard.

"My mama's rules," I answered, grinning to cover my embarrassment.

Doc took the carpetbag from me, lifted it up and down a couple of times, then said, "It's as heavy as an anchor. I'd say it's about time you lightened your load."

"Already have," I said, holding out the legs of my trousers, crossing my bare feet, and doing a little curtsy.

The fog thinned by nine, the sky shone the blue of Jon-Jacob's eyes by ten, and soon we were heading upriver. We had hoped to make it as far as Dubuque, where Doc was anxious to run some kind of secret errand, but with the late start we made it only as far as Nine Mile Island by nightfall—too dark for photographs.

We arrived at the busy Dubuque harbor by midmorning the next day, and since Doc said he'd not be long on his errand, we didn't bother to bleed off the steam in the boiler. When he returned, out of breath, perspiring, and red-faced, he was toting a large box and grinning like a little boy who had just discovered a stick of peppermint in his Christmas stocking. "I cleaned out the mercantile's stock of photographic supplies," he said. "Now you can—I mean, we can—take as many photographs as we'd like."

* * *

Just north of Dubuque, the eastern shore of the river became Wisconsin. There wasn't anything to mark this change, like the Missouri River had marked the border between Nebraska and Iowa, and the Mississippi River divided Iowa from Illinois. It was Wisconsin simply because it said so on the navigation charts.

That evening, a bit upriver from Guttenberg, Iowa, I photographed Hannah and Jon-Jacob standing on the shore, the *Oh My* in the background. I would have included Isaac except that he said he'd rather wait until he could stand on his own two feet. Reluctantly, I allowed Doc to take my photograph. The photograph of Jon-Jacob and Hannah turned out beautifully. Mine, on the other hand, flopped. Doc must have jiggled the camera when removing the lens cap, because my negative came out unrecognizably blurry. "You captured me perfectly," I said, hoping to make light of his failed attempt. But that was the last photograph Doc took with the Eclipse No. 3.

The Eclipse No. 3 stayed in its case the next evening and the next. Where before we had tied up by midafternoon, we now pushed on until six or seven. If Hannah were to make it to St. Paul in time, we needed to keep moving. And pushing harder meant the boiler ate twice as much wood. While Hannah, Doc, and I cut and split and hauled, Isaac and Jon-Jacob scratched their heads in the boiler room. One of the boiler pipes had sprung a hissing leak.

They settled for a quick fix—a drip bucket and a thick bandage of rags, like that covering Isaac's leg.

Time was running out for me too. If we kept up this pace, we'd make Winona in two or three days. In two or three days, we'd be saying our goodbyes to Doc. In two or three days, I'd be saying goodbye to the Eclipse No. 3. I practiced taking photographs with my eye. A leaning willow with its skirt of weeping branches was a fine lady, bending to study her reflection in the river. A cottonwood growing so close to the bank that half its roots were exposed was an old man, cupping his arthritic hands to drink.

DR. MILLER'S HOME BURGLARIZED

ROCK ISLAND, ILLINOIS—
Dr. Matthew Miller returned from Chicago to find that his summer home had been burglarized. Taken were a medical bag, several vials of medicinal powders, bandages, medical books, fishing gear, a suit of clothing, and his beloved fishing boat. Several rivermen reported seeing a small stern-wheeler tied up at Dr. Miller's dock this past Tuesday evening. Two women and a young boy were seen swimming nearby. Also wanted for questioning is Dr. Miller's handyman and former patient—a Mr. James Downy, who suffers from delusions of grandeur and has, in the past, represented himself as a dentist, a lawyer, and a circuit judge. Anyone with information about this theft is asked to contact the Rock Island authorities.

Chapter 28

PRAIRIE OF THE DOG

A SHORT DISTANCE SOUTH OF PRAIRIE DU CHIEN, WISCONSIN, I WAS focused on finding the marker for the Wisconsin River. "Marker coming up," I said when I finally spotted it.

Hannah leaned forward as if straining to see. "Where?" she asked.

"Just there," I answered, pointing.

"Either I need eyeglasses or you've been blessed with the vision of a hawk," she said.

"I've had lots of practice."

Hannah thought on that and then smiled. "You're a wonder, Megan. A true wonder."

"That makes two of us, then."

"Yep, the wonder sisters of Prairie Hill."

✽   ✽   ✽

Prairie Hill and Prairie du Chien. Sisters of another sort, though Prairie Hill didn't have a true hill, only a slight rise at its center, and Prairie du Chien didn't have a true prairie, where grasslands spread from horizon to horizon. Prairie du Chien was skirted by towering bluffs.

There was quite a lot of river traffic, so I held my question about the name of the city until it was behind us. Hannah had more than an answer—she had a history. It had once been a camping place for a Fox Indian chief whose name was "the Dog." Later, after the French fur traders settled there, they'd named it Prairie du Chien, which in French meant "prairie of the dog." A back channel divided Prairie du Chien proper from St. Feriole Island, where many of the residents still spoke French. "We spent several enjoyable days on St. Feriole Island last summer. It reminds us of New Orleans. Maybe, if there's time on our return trip, we can stop, stay a couple of days."

The return trip meant I'd be going home. Home to dirty diapers and baskets brimming with laundry to iron. Home without a river holding it up. Home and Mama's rules. I shuddered at the thought, or at least I thought it was me who shuddered until Hannah asked, "What was that?"

I shrugged and, as if on cue, the paddlewheel stopped slapping the water.

"Quick, go below and find out what's happened."

As I lifted the trapdoor, Doc called up. "Pitman yoke busted clean through. Isaac says to turn the rudder hard right, tie it off, and then come on down to the deck and pole."

"Go," Hannah said as she spun the wheel.

I flew.

The *Oh My* was already drifting backward with the current by the time I joined Doc and Jon-Jacob. I helped Doc unlash the extra bamboo measuring poles that were suspended from leather cords under the deck roof, and by the time we'd gotten them to the floor, Hannah and Isaac had joined us. Isaac hobbled on his crutch, and Hannah carried one of the cabin chairs, which she placed near the rail. "Take a pole and space yourself out. We'll try to make the eastern shore," Isaac said.

"Me, too?" Jon-Jacob asked, and then frosted his plea by adding, "Please, please, Papa, I'm big enough."

"You, too, son," Isaac answered.

Getting ourselves and our poles into place might have seemed comical to us if we hadn't been in an emergency. The portside deck was quite narrow and was made even narrower by the pyramids of cut wood that we'd stacked there. Hannah sent one stack rolling after she bumped into it, and Doc almost poked out his eye on the tip of my pole.

Isaac, stationed on the chair and wielding a pole of his own, became, as Doc put it, our coxswain. "Poles down. Push-push-push.

Poles up. Poles down. Push-push-push. Poles up," he chanted. Except for his voice, all was eerily silent. No drumbeat of the engine; no paddlewheel pounding the water. "Poles down. Push-push-push. Poles up." Over and over as the current swept us past landmarks we'd passed only minutes before. "Poles down. Push-push-push. Poles up."

There was no way to measure our progress, because the shore we were poling to reach was at our backs. Push-push-push.

It didn't take long for me, with my aching arms, to wonder if we'd ever break free of the current. "Poles down. Push-push-push. Poles up. Poles down. Push-push-push. Poles up."

Isaac's voice began to weaken, and with a nod to Hannah he passed the coxswain's role to her. She didn't miss a beat. Her voice, higher than Isaac's, wasn't as commanding, but the change was refreshing and made me feel like we were starting over again. My pushes were stronger; the ache nearly forgotten. "Poles down. Push-push-push. Poles up. Poles down. Push-push-push. Poles up."

Jon-Jacob was the only one of the five who didn't rain with perspiration, and he was also alone in the wide grin he wore. I knew well what he was feeling, like the first time Mama had allowed me to carry the bucket of freshly separated cream. It didn't matter that my arms felt like they were being pulled out of their shoulder sockets. It didn't matter that the palms of my hands burned from gripping the bucket handle. What mattered was that I'd been given a grownup's responsibility, and that was enough. "Poles down. Push-push-push. Poles up. Poles down. Push-push-push. Poles up."

And then, so gradually that I wasn't sure if it was really happening, our poles found bottom more quickly. And then quicker still, and the *Oh My*, finally pushing free of the channel, slowed.

Hannah nodded to me and I took up the chant. "Poles down. Push-push-push. Poles up. Poles down. Push-push-push. Poles up." It was a chant heard and then spoken so often that day, it stuck in my head and replayed itself repeatedly in the weeks and months to follow.

Once I had the rhythm going, Hannah laid down her pole. "I'll go around to the other side, see if there are any hazards between us and the shore."

With our luck, it wasn't a surprise when Hannah hollered back, "Slow the chant by half. There's a snag."

So I slowed the chant by doubling the words, saying one out loud and the other in my head. "Poles *poles* down *down*. Push *push* push *push* push *push*. Poles *poles* up *up*."

After what seemed an eternity, though was probably only ten minutes, Hannah poked her head around from the front deck. "Perfect pace. We missed the snag by a good fifteen feet. Prairie du Chien coming up. We should come ashore at the northern tip of St. Feriole Island."

I nodded in time to the push-push-push.

* * *

There was plenty of cheering and backslapping when the *Oh My* was safely tied to shore. The tin of udder balm we passed from one to the other, salving our blistered hands, could just as easily have been a bottle of dandelion wine.

Our celebration ended soon enough, though.

A fellow stepped out of a nearby house that was built from logs. "Can't tie up here," he shouted. "This is private property."

Doc leapt down from the *Oh My* and approached the man. They stood in private conversation. Hands gesturing wildly, and then, after a time, the gesturing quieted into a handshake. When Doc returned, a big smile was plastered on his face. "Fellow changed his mind. Says you can stay tied up here for as long as you like."

"How did you convince him?" Isaac asked.

Doc winked. "Sometimes a man has to have his secrets."

Later, after returning the poles to their lashings, we gathered about the cabin table, soothing our hands on warm cups of tea Hannah had flavored with cinnamon. "Can the Pitman yoke be repaired?" Hannah asked.

Isaac shook his head. "It needs to be all of one piece, and ours snapped clean in two."

"Perhaps there's a foundry here in Prairie du Chien that could forge a new one."

"Even if there is, they'd want a passel of money, more than we can afford."

Hannah leaned back in her chair.

"But I have another idea. There's a Pitman yoke that should fit the *Oh My* in the salvaged parts pile back home at the boatworks. All I have to do is send a telegram to Mr. Gluck and ask him to find a river pilot willing to haul it upriver."

Hannah leaned forward again. "How long might that take?"

"Weeks, I'm afraid."

"Then I need to send a telegram up to St. Paul, inform Mr. Wallencott that he will have to direct my play without me."

"Whoa," Isaac said. "The *Oh My* is stuck here, and I'm stuck here, but that doesn't mean you are. This is all my fault. If I hadn't insisted that we stop to help those fellows free the logjam, I wouldn't have bunged up my leg and we'd be in St. Paul by now. You've got to go, Hannah, or I'll never forgive myself. You and Jon-Jacob and Megan should go on ahead."

"I'll not leave you here by yourself. What if your health takes a turn for the worse after I'm gone?"

"How long will you need to be up in St. Paul?" Doc asked.

"Nearly four weeks. But if you're thinking what I think you're thinking, we can't and won't impose on your generosity one moment longer than we already have."

"It wouldn't be an imposition to stay long enough to see that the infection isn't coming back. It's looking so good at this point, I think we can stop with the maggots and leeches."

"See there," Isaac said. "You don't have a thing to worry about."

"And what about after Doc leaves? Who will go into town to fetch fresh milk and whatever else you'll need from the grocer?"

"I can stay with Isaac," I said.

"Mama would wring my neck," Hannah shot back.

"Then we'll not tell her, at least until we're all back together again."

"No. No. No. This is all wrong," Hannah said. "You're all talking crazy. Besides, if I spend the little money we have left on railway tickets, we'll be flat broke."

"It's not crazy," Isaac said. "I'm thinking that in a couple of days I might feel up to doing a little carpentry work. Town this size, there's bound to be someone who needs some custom woodworking."

I didn't let Isaac's idea grow any grass before adding my own. "And there ought to be some kind of paid work that I can do, when I'm not taking care of things here on the *Oh My*, that is." This was my chance to finally fess up about needing to earn my ticket home, and I might have, if not for Jon-Jacob. "Me, too," he chimed in. "I'll get me a job poling rafts."

Hannah ruffled Jon-Jacob's hair. "I'll just bet you would, but if I go, and that's a very big if, then who will take care of me up in St. Paul?"

"Me?"

"None other."

Jon-Jacob beamed.

Isaac worked on Hannah for another hour, bombarding her with convincing arguments. The last string weren't convincing so much as they were funny. "If you don't go, then Mr. Wallencott will make a mess of your play, and he'll be tarred and feathered and driven out of town on a rail, and then he'll blame you and forbid you from coming in to clean his house, and the clutter and dust will pile up and up and up, and then one day we'll read in the newspapers that he suffocated to death. Now, you wouldn't want to be responsible for killing that nice fellow, would you?"

"You're never going to let me rest, are you?" Hannah asked.

"It's the right thing to do, Hannah."

"Okay, I'll go, but only if you promise to send a telegram if I'm needed here, for any reason."

"I promise," Isaac answered.

"You've got to cross your heart and hope to die, else the promise isn't any good," Jon-Jacob said.

"I know something even better than crossing my heart. It's called sealing a promise with a kiss," Isaac said.

Hannah obliged.

Chapter 19

AROUND TOWN

HANNAH ASKED ME TO ACCOMPANY HER TO THE CHICAGO, MILWAUKEE, and St. Paul railway station, where she would purchase her tickets and send a telegram to Isaac's boss in New Orleans. The bicycle had gone unused since I'd come aboard in Burlington, but Hannah thought I might find it useful for getting around St. Feriole Island. I'd have the distance to the station and back to learn how to ride it.

I'd never worn the trousers in public, though I was glad for them when I hoisted my leg over the bar. "Place one foot on the highest pedal, and push off with the other. Once you're rolling, begin to pedal. The secret to steering is in the handlebars. If you feel yourself losing balance, steer in the direction of the fall."

I pushed off. I pedaled. I fell. I dusted myself off, got back on, pushed and pedaled, wobbled maybe five feet and fell again. Again and again, my pride scraped and bruised as my skin was surely going to be. "Remember about the steering," Hannah reminded me each time she helped me up. And then . . . I was riding, fast! Too fast! "How do I stop?" I shouted over my shoulder.

"Reverse the pedals."

I reversed too hard and jolted myself to the ground.

Hannah ran to catch up. "Sorry. I forgot to tell you how to stop. That's probably enough for one day. You'll have time to practice on your own once I'm gone."

As we walked the bike along Water Street, Hannah pointed off to the left. "That's Villa Louis. Isn't it grand?"

It was a grand home, with its three stories and porches all around, its bricked paths and manicured lawns, its tidy outbuildings and ponds. "Very grand. But I'll bet it doesn't have a rudder," I said.

Hannah chuckled. "Why, Megan. You've become a true river rat."

"Rat?"

"It's just a phrase that describes people who prefer living on the water to living on the land."

I imagined myself with a hairless tail, beady eyes, and whiskers.

There were several stone structures lining the next block—the Brisbois Store and two rather large homes, though it was the building at the corner of Water and Fisher that truly caught my eye—the Dousmen House Hotel. Six chimneys and four stories of arched windows lined the Fisher Street side. Fronting Water Street were more arched windows, these looking out upon the river. Wide stairs led from the street to a covered entrance. Atop it all, as if a crown, sat a large cupola.

I'd never spent the night in a hotel, large or small, but from the number of windows, I guessed the Dousmen House had at least a hundred rooms. A hundred beds. A hundred sets of sheets, to say nothing of towels and facecloths. There was a laundry somewhere in that building. If they'd have me, I'd earn my way home as a laundress!

I waited with the bicycle outside the station while Hannah went inside. Two young women, shading themselves with parasols, strolled past. They looked my way. I nodded. As they walked away, they giggled into their hands. I had to fight a strong urge to follow after them, explain about the trousers. I stayed put. They wouldn't understand, like Mama wouldn't understand, like I wouldn't have understood before falling overboard. There was a price to be paid for wearing trousers, and I'd just made an installment.

After an early supper, Doc, saying he wanted to see what kind of entertainment Prairie du Chien had to offer, dressed himself in a dapper suit he'd packed in his duffle and set off for town.

It being my last chance to photograph Hannah, Isaac, and Jon-Jacob as a family, I busied myself in preparation. The bandages on

Isaac's leg didn't say a thing about who he really was, so I'd decided to frame the three from the waist up. I'd sit Isaac in a chair, with Hannah and Jon-Jacob standing at his side.

Hannah busied herself, too. She sewed a button on Jon-Jacob's best shirt, scrubbed his face rosy, and ran a wet comb through his hair. She'd brushed, rolled, and pinned her own hair into a chignon, and was about to take the scissors to Isaac's beard when Isaac leaned away and said, "Nobody will recognize us, all spiffed up."

Hannah thought on that for a moment, laid the scissors aside, and then removed her hairpins and shook her head until her hair fell over her shoulders. She curled a finger at Jon-Jacob, and when he came to her, she unbuttoned the top button on his shirt and ruffled his hair.

Isaac patted Hannah's rear and said, "Now, that's more like it."

Hannah and Isaac were still in their playful moods when I positioned them for the photograph. And playful is what I captured when I pulled the lens cap away. All three smiled, the moment's happiness shining in their eyes. There, behind the camera, I felt something I hadn't felt when taking the earlier photographs. I felt privileged to share in their moment.

I developed two photographs from the negative. One for Hannah and another for Mama. I'd need a peace offering for not having written as many letters as Mama had made me promise to write, and the photograph, which both Hannah and I thought to be my best, would do just fine. Just fine indeed.

Later, Hannah retrieved a long box from the far reaches under her bed. After removing the dusty lid and folding back a layer of tissue paper, she found that the summer-weight wool suit she'd brought along to wear to the theater had been munched on by moths. "That settles it, I'm not going," she said.

"I'm sure Lila wouldn't mind if you wore her wedding suit," I offered, though I expected that Lila would, indeed, mind. "All I ask is that you return it—uncrushed, unstained, untorn, un-rained-on, un-anything."

Hannah smiled knowingly.

And when I saw that Hannah was intending to pack her and Jon-Jacob's things into a flour sack, I offered up Mama's carpetbag. And while I was at it, I offered up Hester's spare pair of shoes and Mama's blue hat.

"Isn't that the hat you used to wear when you went into Prairie Hill?" Isaac asked Hannah.

"Same one," Hannah answered.

Isaac grinned. "Would you mind putting it on?"

Hannah raised the hat to her head.

Isaac let out a whistle. "Look there, son, that's the way your mama looked the day I fell in love with her."

Jon-Jacob tried to whistle, too, but all he made was air.

"Don't worry, son. When the right gal comes along, your whistler will work just fine."

"What are you teaching my son?"

"Man stuff." Isaac pulled out his harmonica then and played an especially lilting tune. Hannah was quick to smile, and Jon-Jacob clapped his hands.

When Isaac put his harmonica away, Jon-Jacob climbed into Isaac's lap. "Tell me the story again, Papa, about how you made up that music watching Mama dance on the prairie."

Isaac faked dismay. "But I've told you that story a hundred times."

"Tell it again, Papa. Please."

Isaac rumpled Jon-Jacob's hair, and began. Though I went through the motions of wiping up the spattered grease from the stove, I was as intent as Jon-Jacob to hear Isaac's story.

"Well, when I was a young man, I spent my days plowing up the prairie sod. One day, I looked up and spied your mama making her way through the knee-high grass. She was the picture of pretty, the easy way she moved, the sun and wind playing in her hair. So pretty that I was smitten right there on the spot. So smitten that I whoaed the team and pulled my harmonica out of my pocket and made up a tune to match your mama."

"And you called it Hannah Music," Jon-Jacob added.

"That's right, son. Hannah Music. But I played it soft so your mama wouldn't hear. You know how your mama is; if she'd known that I was watching, she'd have skedaddled."

"Tell the part about Mama looking for a shining thing. Please, Papa, tell that part next."

"I was just getting to that. Your mama would slow now and again and raise her hand to her brow as if she was searching for some shining thing off in the distance."

Jon-Jacob turned to Hannah. "Now it's your turn, Mama. Your turn to tell what the shining thing was."

"Let's see if I can remember. A turtle?"

"No, Mama. It wasn't a turtle."

"A goose then?"

"Not a goose."

"Oh, that's right, I remember now. That shining thing I was looking into the future for was *you*."

Jon-Jacob squealed with glee.

The next morning, when Hannah discovered that Doc's bed hadn't been slept in, she again said, "That's it. I'm not going."

Doc appeared at the cabin doorway, a newspaper tucked under his arm, just as Hannah was about to begin unpacking Mama's carpetbag. "Sorry, I met a fellow, an old friend, and we stayed up all night reminiscing." He wished Hannah a good and safe trip, shook hands with Jon-Jacob, and then disappeared into the boiler room. I'd not heard Doc snore in his time on the *Oh My*. He snored that morning, loud and echoing like thunder, and Hannah closed the carpetbag.

I'd dressed in the least tattered of my everyday shirtwaists and least tattered of my everyday skirts and used the best-I-could-do spit polish on my everyday shoes. Isaac gave me two things—a handwritten notice he wanted me to post at the local lumberyard and an example of his woodworking skills, an ornate piece of handcarved fretwork.

I excused myself and waited on the deck while Hannah and Jon-Jacob said their goodbyes to Isaac. Both had tears in their eyes when they joined me, which brought tears to mine.

As we walked along the path toward town, I buried my nervousness over Hannah leaving by burying her with questions, though never so rapid-fire as when we were passing the Dousmen House Hotel. How long would it take for the train to carry them from Prairie du Chien to St. Paul? Eight or nine hours. How would they get from the St. Paul railway station to the Wallencott home? Jon-Jacob answered that one—they'd take a newfangled electric street trolley. What would they do when not at the theater? "Miss you and Isaac terribly," Hannah answered.

The train whistled into the station just as we arrived. I was almost glad for this. After my experience at the station in Prairie Hill, I didn't relish a long goodbye, for Hannah or for myself. We settled for hugs, and then they boarded.

Once inside and seated, Hannah and Jon-Jacob waved from the coach car windows, and I tasted a little of what I guessed Mama had felt when she'd stood on the platform back in Prairie Hill. Being the one left behind was bittersweet. It was as if I was saying goodbye to part of myself.

Chapter 20

LOOKING FOR WORK

ONCE HANNAH'S TRAIN HAD LEFT THE STATION, I HURRIED OFF IN THE direction Isaac had said he remembered there being a lumberyard. I found it just where Isaac had said I would and went into the office. The man behind the desk was only a clerk, who said he couldn't speak for the owner, but that if I left the notice and the fretwork, he'd make sure that the owner saw it. I had my doubts.

That left the Dousmen House Hotel. I didn't know much about applying for a job, though I knew enough to go around back instead of climbing the steps at the front entrance. A girl about my age was pegging damp sheets to a clothesline. "Excuse me, miss. Could you tell me who I need to see about employment?"

The girl straightened her back. "That'd be Mrs. Kingsley, but she's in an awful foul mood today. You might want to think about coming back tomorrow, or better yet, next week."

"Thank you for the advice, but I need to find work as soon as possible. Could you tell me where I might find her?"

"You can't say I didn't warn you. Laundry is through that door and down the hall to the right."

I braced myself with several deep breaths, put one foot in front of the other, and was soon standing in a cloud of steam that reminded me of the fog on the river, where I would much rather have been at that moment.

I cleared my throat in the way one does when one wants to get noticed. Mrs. Kingsley didn't notice, so I walked up to where she was feeding sheets through the ringer. "Excuse me, ma'am. Might you be Mrs. Kingsley?"

Mrs. Kingsley, a rather round woman, looked up and scowled.

"Might be. Depends on why you're asking."

"I'm looking for employment, ma'am."

She finished wringing the bedsheet and wiped her hands on her apron. "There might be work here, for the right girl."

Hope clapped its hands in my heart.

"You live here on the island?" she asked.

"For the time being."

"Either you live here or you don't."

"I've been traveling on the river with my sister and her husband and our boat broke down and it looks like we'll be here for a while."

She waved her hand as if to tell me to go away. "Don't be wasting my time then. I only hire local girls, girls who come from good Christian families."

"I come from a good family, ma'am, truly I do, and if you'd only give me a chance, I promise that I'll work twice as hard as anyone else."

"Good families don't allow their daughters to associate with river riffraff."

"With all due respect, ma'am, not everyone on the river is riffraff. My sister and her husband are good people, as good as they come."

"Listen, missy. Don't you be trying to tell me about river people. I've lived next to this river all my life, and I know what I know."

"You don't know my sister and her husband, and you don't know me," I said, deliberately leaving off the *ma'am* because Mrs. Kingsley didn't deserve it. I was about to say more, but stopped myself. Her mind was closed, like a door with a rusty lock.

As I hurried out, I passed the girl who had been hanging sheets. "Told you so," she snickered.

I didn't much like this girl, either, but she had been honest with me, even if I hadn't listened. "Are there any other establishments in town that might be hiring?" I asked.

She shook her head. "If there were, I'd be working there instead of here."

"Don't you be wasting my girl's time," Mrs. Kingsley's voice bounded across the yard. "You go on and scat now," she said as if I was nothing more than a stray cat.

Holding my head high, I walked away, slow as if on a Sunday stroll. My head sank back into my shoulders, though, when I turned the corner.

I walked and thought, walked and thought. At Fourth and Brisbois, I passed a small house with a baby pram parked on the porch. This gave me an idea. I walked up the steps and rapped on the door. The woman who answered my knock was holding a baby, and two young children peered out from behind her skirts. "I'm sorry to bother you, ma'am, but I was wondering if you might be in need of a mother's helper. I have quite a lot of experience and am willing to work for a modest amount."

"Je ne parle pas anglais," she said, the lilt of her voice like a song.

"I'm sorry, ma'am, but I don't understand."

The tallest of the children, a girl about Jon-Jacob's age, stepped forward. "My mama speaks only French."

"Tell your mother that I'm so sorry I bothered her."

The girl spoke a fairly long string of French words to her mother and the mother spoke some French words back. "Mama says to tell you that you have *beaux yeux*, beautiful eyes."

"How do you say thank you and good day in French?" I asked.

"Merci et bonjour."

"Merci et bonjour," I repeated, then smiled and walked away.

At the next house down, my knock was answered by a frail, white-haired woman. "I'm sorry to bother you, ma'am, but I was wondering if you might be in need of a girl to do the heavy work, the rug beating and such. I have quite a bit of experience and am willing to work for a modest amount."

"My son and daughter-in-law live just up the street. They take care of all the heavy work for me. But if you'd like to come in for a cup of tea, I wouldn't mind some company."

Remembering Mrs. Galt's unending talk on the train, I politely excused myself.

I changed my speech at the next house, which had quite a lot of laundry hanging from the clothesline. "I'm sorry to bother you, ma'am, but I was wondering if you might have any ironing I might do for you. I'd charge but a nickel a garment."

"I might as well tote my basket across the bridge to Haberman's Laundry for that price."

I'd have offered a penny, if she hadn't slammed the door in my face. She'd given me an idea, though, and that was something. I'd tote myself across the bridge and apply for work at Haberman's Laundry.

I headed east, reckoning that I'd see the bridge once I was standing on the banks of the back channel. I was almost to the water at the end of Brisbois Street when two rather unwashed-looking men, one older, one younger, began shouting at one another.

"I've had it," the younger man said. "I might as well be working on a chain gang, splitting rocks with a pickax. You can get someone else to do your dirty work. I quit." The younger man turned then and brushed past me.

"Get back here!" the older man shouted.

The younger man didn't look back.

The older man, shaking his head and muttering to himself, turned and began to walk toward a clutter of ramshackle sheds.

"Sir, may I have a word with you?" I called.

The man stopped, turned, and, seeing that I was the one who had called out, he looked to his right and left as if thinking I must have been addressing someone else in the vicinity. Not seeing anyone else, he pointed a finger at his chest and grinned.

When I reached him, I thrust out my hand and said, "Megan Barnett, sir."

He wiped his hand on his trousers and then took my hand in a hearty shake. "Pierre Beauchamp."

"Might you be looking to hire a helper?"

"Looks that way. Do you know any fellows who might be interested in earning a little money cooking out my clams?"

"What does the work involve?"

"You're not from around here, are you?"

I'd learned my lesson with Mrs. Kingsley. "I've come here only recently."

"Well that explains it. If you were from around here, you'd know something about clamming. I'm a clammer, see, and I need somebody to tend the cooker."

"So you need someone who knows something about keeping and feeding a fire?"

"That, and fast hands for cleaning the meat out of the shells. They should also have a good eye for finding pearls."

"How much are you willing to pay?"

"Well, for the right fellow, someone who's trustworthy, I'd be willing to make the same deal I made with my no-account nephew. I'd split the profits sixty-forty."

"I don't quite understand."

"Button factories pay between eight and twelve dollars a ton, depending on the size and quality of the shells. Whatever I make in a week, I keep sixty percent and my helper keeps the other forty."

"How many tons of shells can you harvest in a day?"

"If I'm working by myself, I can only process three-quarters of a ton in a week. But if I have good help, I can double and sometimes triple that amount."

"I know someone who would love to work for you. A person who is as trustworthy and hard working as they come, and has a very good eye."

"Send him on over to talk to me."

"It's me, sir."

If laughs were peaches, Mr. Beauchamp could have filled a bushel basket.

I waited until the last peach had tumbled out. "I can do the work, sir, if you'll only give me a chance to prove it to you."

"I'd be laughed right off the island, hiring a girl."

"You'll be the one laughing, sir, when I cook and clean more shells than anyone has ever cooked or cleaned. And if there's a pearl to be found, you can be sure that I'll find it for you."

He looked hard at me then, as if he was considering it. "Never work," he said, shaking his head.

"Let me work to the end of the day, for free, and if you're not satisfied, then you can look for someone else."

He looked me up and down. "You'll set yourself on fire, working in those skirts."

"I have trousers, sir. It will only take me a short while to go home and change."

"Where do you live?"

"At the far north end of Water Street."

"I'd best go along, make sure it's okay with your pa."

"I'm living with my brother-in-law."

"Same thing. I want him to know I don't have any bad intentions."

So off we went. I held my breath as the *Oh My* came into view, for fear that Mr. Beauchamp would turn on his heel the moment he realized I was river folk.

"Nice boat," he said. "I've always dreamed of owning something like this myself."

Isaac was in the boiler room, propped on his crutch and tinkering with his woodworking tools. I introduced the two, and gave Isaac the short version of why I'd brought Mr. Beauchamp with me, and then slipped into the pantry to change. And eavesdrop. The two exchanged some small talk about the weather, and then Mr. Beauchamp asked, "So what do you think about this gal here, tending my clam cooker? Think she can handle it?"

"As far as I'm concerned, Megan can do anything she sets her mind to. She's piloted this boat, tended the boiler, cut wood, and she's a mighty fine maggot hunter."

"Maggot hunter?"

"It's a long story. What I'm trying to say is that if I were you, I'd feel mighty lucky that Megan was willing to work for me."

Isaac's words were like bowknots on the tail of a kite, lifting me into the sky.

"I do have a couple of questions for you, though. You'll pay her fair, not try to cheat her out of what she earns?"

"Pay her the same as I paid my nephew, sixty percent for me, forty for her. Fair and square."

"And no foul language."

"I might look like a heathen, but I don't swear and I don't drink, and I go to mass regular-like."

"Sounds to me like you and Megan have a deal then."

I took that as my cue to step into the boiler room. "I'm ready to begin."

Mr. Beauchamp smiled. "I have business I need to attend to down at the steamboat office. Give me half an hour, then meet me back at my place."

When Mr. Beauchamp had gone, Isaac turned to me and said, "Doc's gone."

"Gone?"

"Got up not long after you and Hannah left this morning, poured himself a cup of coffee, then sat down at the table and started in reading that newspaper he brought back with him. He'd flipped a couple of pages. And then it was like his eyes got stuck. Like he was reading the same little piece over and over. Then he ripped that page away from the rest and bolted into the boiler room. I could hear him rustling around, and the next thing I know, he's back, his duffle slung over his shoulder, his eyes looking dull and vacant, and he's saying that he has to leave. He's halfway out the door, when he stops, turns back, and says whatever he's left behind, we should drop it by his house in Rock Island on our way downriver. Everything except the camera. He said you should keep that, and all the paraphernalia that goes along with it. Says it's his gift to you for saving his life. And then he goes to leave again, and stops again, and then says that he's mighty sorry for any trouble that comes our way because of him, and then he left."

Two thoughts fought for space in my head. The Eclipse No. 3 was mine, and trouble. Trouble won out. "What kind of trouble do you suppose he meant?"

Isaac shrugged his shoulders. "I don't have a clue, but I do know one thing. If Hannah knew Doc had skedaddled, she'd be back here on the next train. It's your choice, I'd never ask you to lie, but if you could see your way clear to postponing the truth in your letters to her, I'd be mighty grateful."

"I promised that I'd send a telegram if there was trouble."

"And you will. If trouble comes a calling. As of right now, we're fine. More than fine, in fact. The owner of the lumberyard just left. Guess he was pretty impressed with that piece of fretwork you dropped off, and he wants me to craft a fireplace mantel for the home he's building. He'll be coming by with the wood later today."

Isaac had work, I had work, and the Eclipse No. 3 was mine. *How much finer could it get?*

"It's settled, then?"

"Settled," I answered, then headed off to work—on the bicycle. I fell twice, almost got flattened by a freight wagon whose path I wobbled into, and scared the dickens out of a bent old man who was trying to cross Brisbois Street.

Mr. Beauchamp taught me everything I needed to know about clam cooking that first afternoon, and he was so pleased with how fast I learned, and how fast I worked, that he made it official, and I became Mr. Pierre Beauchamp's clamming partner.

I'd rise early, rain or shine, gobble down the flapjacks Isaac whipped and flipped for me, pack a lunch of whatever leftovers I could scare up from the night before, and then ride off on the bicycle and arrive at Mr. Beauchamp's around six o'clock, just in time to say good morning as he launched his small, flat-bottomed johnboat into the channel. He'd found pearls earlier in the summer, and therefore kept the location of his clam beds secret, even from me. "It's like out in California in 1849," he'd said. "A fellow would find a nugget of gold in a little mountain stream, and the next thing he'd know that stream would be elbow to elbow with prospectors."

I began each day by hauling buckets of water up from the channel and filling the cooker, which was a rectangular metal and wooden box raised to waist height by four legs. I'd build a fire under the cooker, then, when the water steamed, I'd add mussels from the pile Mr. Beauchamp had brought in the evening before. Adding the mussels required the use of a tool that looked like a pitchfork except that its tines were spaced more closely together. Once I'd filled the bottom of the cooker with mussels, I covered them with a length of burlap, then twisted the dial of a crusty kitchen timer, setting it at twenty minutes. When the timer dinged, I forked the mussels onto a makeshift table to cool, and then filled the cooker with a second batch. In the twenty minutes it took to cook the next batch, I'd thrust a knife into each mussel's jaw, pry its jaws apart, and then reach inside with my index finger to remove the slimy meat. I rolled this meat between my finger and thumb, feeling for a pearl. The meat, which people thought too foul to eat, I tossed into a bucket, which local farmers collected and fed to their hogs. The shells I deposited, carefully, into one of three handcarts, depending on their size. Then I'd start in on the next mussel, the next batch, over and over until Mr. Beauchamp returned with that day's catch.

When the fire dwindled, I fed it kindling. When the water in the cooker evaporated, I fetched another bucket up from the river. By the end of my first full day, I was beginning to understand why Mr. Beauchamp's nephew had up and quit. My muscles ached, and the mussels, their outsides roughly and darkly ridged and the seams of their jaws sharp as razors, had scraped and cut my hands. The inner surface of the shells, hidden until I opened them to the light, made up for the pain, a little. The insides were silky smooth and iridescent white.

MAN FINDS SIZABLE PEARL

ROCK ISLAND, ILLINOIS—A young man, who wishes to remain anonymous, has found a sizable pearl in the vicinity of Rock Island. "First shell I ever opened, and there it was," the finder claimed. When asked what his plans were for the money, he answered that he'd been following the trail of a young woman and that he would use as much of his newly acquired funds as it took to find her. The obviously smitten young man would also not reveal the location where the mussel shell was found, so please do not phone or stop by the newspaper office. If the location were known to us, this reporter would be out digging for himself.

Chapter 21

PEARL DREAMS

IT WAS HOPE OF FINDING A PEARL THAT KEPT ME GOING. IF NOT IN THE mussel I was holding, then the next or the next or the next. Once I got the routine down, there was more time for thinking as I worked, and I spent most of the thinking time planning how I'd spend the fortune I'd make when I found a pearl. I'd set half aside for the future and spend the rest. I'd buy a book on the latest methods of photography. I'd waltz into a dress shop and ask to see the latest in their ready-made fashions, deck myself out from head to toe in silk and lace. I'd buy a spritzer of flowery French perfume. The perfume daydream usually played out in the late afternoon when, soaked in mussel meat slime, I could barely stand to smell myself.

I'd buy gifts for everyone back home. A new hat for Mama, a pocket watch for Papa, and pairs of fur-lined leather gloves for all the rest. If the pearl were enormous, I'd rent a storefront in Prairie Hill and set up my own photographic studio. And if it were super stupendous, one day I might buy one of Horace's automobiles and drive it around the country taking photographs of nature's moods. Rivers and mountains, deserts and seashores.

I did take one break each day. After washing up as best I could at the cistern pump inside the ramshackle shed where Mr. Beauchamp lived, I'd gobble down my lunch, then, bound for the post office in Prairie du Chien proper, I'd pedal and weave through the wagon and carriage traffic on the busy Bridge Street bridge. Going to the post office was always unpleasant, though never more so than on the first day when I walked my mussel-scented trousers inside. One woman turned to another and whispered behind her white glove. A girl, wearing a starched pinafore, tugged at her mother's skirts and pointed. The postal clerk pleated his brow when I stepped up to the window to buy a postage stamp for the letter I'd written to Mama and to inquire about setting up a temporary box for receiving mail.

I returned each day, to mail letters Isaac and I had written to Hannah or to collect any she had written to us. It did get easier, once I figured out that if I didn't look at the people who were giving me looks, then their looks didn't sting quite so much. And the huge, toothy grin I plastered on my face worked well on the one person I had to look at. The postal clerk, who was a rather dour-faced fellow when waiting on those in line in front of me, would look up, see my grin, and grin big back, as if grins were catching.

On Saturdays, Mr. Beauchamp clammed his secret mussel beds only until midday so he could be on hand when the shell buyer came around. I'd keep cooking or prying or feeling for pearls while Mr. Beauchamp haggled with the buyer. When they'd shaken hands over a price, the buyer carted the shells away. The shells' first stop, as Mr. Beauchamp explained it to me, would be at one of the local button factories, where round saws were used to cut blanks or circular pieces from the shells. The "holey" shells were discarded into mountainous piles, for later use in a variety of ways—from surfacing roads to ground chicken feed. The blanks were loaded on barges and sent downriver to button-finishing factories in Muscatine or upriver to Lansing, Iowa. At the finishing factories, the blanks were ground smooth on a traveling band that passed under grindstones, after which two small holes were drilled for the thread. The buttons were then polished with pumice stone and water in revolving kegs, sorted, and sewed onto cards. Like me, the clams I cooked out that summer really got around.

Saturdays, after the shell buyer drove away, Mr. Beauchamp counted out my share of the earnings into my open palm. One . . . two . . . three . . . that first short week alone. He paid me in paper bills, though they felt the weight of gold tucked away in my trouser pocket.

Evenings, Isaac and I often ate what he called "chef's delight," which meant any crazy combination that we felt like cooking, or not cooking. Jerked beef dipped in orange marmalade; fried oatmeal with dilled pickle spears on the side. After supper, I'd rinse the smell out of the trousers and shirt I'd worn that day, hang them up on the roof to dry, write a few lines in my ongoing letters to Hannah, then, having run out of steam, I'd join Isaac on the deck. The last boats of the evening would pass and, across the river, the lights of McGregor, Iowa, would twinkle on while we talked or read Hannah's letters to one another, again and again. Talking was like our scarecrow, keeping the loneliness birds away. Isaac had it worse than me. One evening, when Isaac didn't know I was watching, he buried his nose in Hannah's pillow and breathed deep breaths. Other times, he might spend the whole evening turning Jon-Jacob's straw fishing hat around and around in his hands. After Hannah left, Isaac took to sleeping on the padded woodbin, saying that the cabin bed was too empty without Hannah in it. Watching Isaac missing Hannah and Jon-Jacob in these ways always made me think of Horace. I'd imagine that he had merely gone away for a few weeks and that we'd be reunited soon. This was silly, and I knew it, but I figured there wasn't any harm in dreaming.

Mr. Beauchamp, true to his word, was a churchgoing man, so I did not work on Sundays. I'd rise just as early, though, to bake the week's bread, harvest whichever vegetable had come ripe in the rooftop garden, pick out the weeds, or do whatever chore needed done that required climbing or a great deal of time spent on one's feet. There was a Methodist church on St. Feriole Island that I could have attended, but I had no decent shoes to wear. Mine were near ruin by then. So I worshiped in another way—by taking photographs of God's handiwork. I was miserly with the dry plates, though. Not knowing when or if I'd be able to purchase more, I kept myself to three a week. The river at dawn. The river at dusk. The river at midday. I wanted to capture what Mr. Greenwald had captured—the river in its ever-changing moods. I came close, in the photograph of an egret, standing so still in the shallows, the S-shaped curve of its neck so unmoving I was able to hold the cap away from the lens for a full fifteen seconds without blur. I was so pleased with the results that I gave the photograph a name—Egret in Calm.

Chapter 22

CHANCE MEETING

THE SUNDAY OF OUR SECOND WEEK ON ST. FERIOLE ISLAND WAS THE
hottest and muggiest day in my recollection, and made even hotter
by my bread making. I'd just removed the last loaf from the oven
when a steamboat whistled its landing. I mopped the perspiration
from my brow, changed into skirts, laced on my shoes, grabbed the
Eclipse No. 3's case, and hurried off to the steamboat landing. I had
hoped the whistle belonged to one of the grand excursion steamers,
with its decks festooned with American flags and well-dressed passengers. But it was just the *Mary Morton,* riding low in the water, her
decks stacked high with sacks, crates, and barrels of goods. There
were a few passengers fanning themselves in the shade of an upper
deck, and a handful of others ambling across the boarding stage. I
was there. The camera was there. I hadn't taken a photograph of a

large steamboat, so I opened the case and set about readying the Eclipse No. 3.

A few minutes later, my eye to the viewfinder, a male voice said, "That's quite the camera."

I looked up and couldn't believe my eyes. Gladness quickened my heart the way it does when you see a friend you haven't seen for a while, especially a friend you never expected to see again. "Seth!" I said.

An expression that read more of panic than recognition swept over Seth's eyes.

He tugged his cap down low. "I'm sorry, miss. You must have mistaken me for someone else." Seth turned then and, taking long strides, headed up the path toward the steamboat office.

"You scared off a thief who was rifling through my bag at the Burlington railway station," I called after him.

He stopped then, and turned, and smiled the most charming of smiles. "That's right. I remember now. That thief made off with your railway ticket."

"Yes, and I gave you a dollar to buy my lunch, but my sister came for me before you returned."

Seth retraced his steps. "As a gentleman, I'd like to return your dollar, but I've been down on my luck and don't have a penny to my name," he said, turning his trouser pockets inside out.

Seth then shifted his attention to the Eclipse No. 3. "I don't recall that you had a camera case among your bags when you were down in Burlington. You must have come into some money since then."

"I am working, trying to earn enough money to purchase another ticket, but the camera was a gift."

"From a gentleman?"

"Yes."

"Bet you sweet-talked him out of it."

Unease dented my glad. "It wasn't like that at all. It was a gift for saving the man's life."

"Well, aren't you full of surprises. A genuine Florence Nightingale." Seth then wiped perspiration from his forehead with a sleeve and said, "I could use a little saving myself. I haven't eaten a proper meal in a couple of days. That, combined with this heat, is making me a little woozy."

I remembered woozy, and Seth did look a little pale. My unease gave way to sisterly concern. Seth had been a friend to me when I'd needed one. Returning the favor seemed the least I could do. "My brother-in-law's boat is tied up not far from here. If you don't mind waiting until I put the camera away, I'll take you there and make you something to eat."

A bit of color returned to Seth's cheeks. "I'd be beholden."

Once the Eclipse No. 3 was back inside its case, Seth reached for the handle. "Here, the least I can do is carry the case for you."

I held tight. "That's kind of you, but I prefer carrying it myself."

Seth threw his hands up in the air. "Whatever you say."

Seth chattered on and on about his bad luck as we walked along Water Street. He'd not been able to find work, at least none that had suited him, in all the time that had passed since we'd last met. I wondered privately how he'd gained passage on the *Mary Morton* and was in fact thinking to ask just that question when, passing the Dousmen House Hotel, Seth, complaining anew about the heat, began rolling up his sleeves. I happened to glance at his arms and what I saw there made my blood run cold. A tattoo of a dancing girl! I stopped walking as suddenly as if someone had lowered a larger-than-life WANTED poster out of the sky.

Acting the fool had happened slow. Realizing that I'd been one happened as quickly and stingingly as a slap. Seth was Samuel. It all fit. Seth hadn't chased off a thief, he'd been the one who'd stolen my railway ticket. And the ticket agent. It was my ticket Seth had passed through the bars, my money that he'd slipped into his pocket. And I knew then that I could have waited in the Burlington station until I was covered with cobwebs and my hair turned gray before I'd have seen that slice of ham.

"I . . . I just remembered that I . . . I promised a friend who lives at the hotel that I'd drop something off this afternoon." I patted my pocket for added believability.

"I'll come along then."

"My friend is ill, and I wouldn't want you to expose yourself. You'll be more comfortable if you wait over there on that shaded bench."

"You won't be long, will you?"

"Not long at all."

I ran up the hotel's front steps, the Eclipse No. 3's case thumping against my leg. It took a moment for my eyes to adjust to the stale darkness of the lobby. When the blur lifted I marched up to the front desk. "Do you have a telephone?" I asked the clerk.

"We do, but it's only for the use of staff and guests."

"Could you place a call for me then? This is an emergency."

The desk clerk frowned over the top of his half-moon spectacles. "What kind of an emergency?"

"There's a man outside, and he's an escapee from the Fort Madison Jail."

"You sure? Don't want to pull the constable away from his Sunday dinner for a wild goose chase."

"I'm sure."

The desk clerk turned the phone's crank several times, put the receiver to his ear, and then spoke into the mouthpiece. "Hazel, this is Abe down at the Dousmen. I need you to ring up the constable for me."

I couldn't see Seth from the front desk, so I moved closer to one of the lace-curtained windows. He was still sitting on the bench.

"Yes, I know it's Sunday, but I've got a gal here who claims to have spotted a fellow who escaped from the Fort Madison Jail." He leaned away from the mouthpiece. "What's the fellow's name?"

"Samuel Silver, though he also goes by Seth Martin."

Abe repeated the names into the telephone and then lowered the mouthpiece. "Where's this Silver fellow right now?"

"Sitting on a bench across the street."

"Sitting on a bench across the street from the hotel. . . . Okay, I'll tell her." Abe hung up the receiver then. "Constable says he's coming right down and that you're to stay put."

I nodded, then returned my attention to the window. Seth was on his feet, pacing back and forth.

Abe walked around the desk and joined me. "Doesn't look like a criminal."

"Looks can be deceiving."

Two nicely dressed young women, probably on their way home from church, strolled by about then, and Seth flashed that white-toothed smile of his and tipped his cap. He said something, and the shorter of the two giggled into her gloved hands. And then Seth said something else and the taller of the girls took the arm of the other and hurried her along the sidewalk. I'd never know the taller girl's name, never have a chance to chat with her, but she hadn't been fooled, and I admired her for that.

Seth stood there, watching the girls walk away, then turned toward the hotel and began crossing the street. By the time his footsteps creaked the lobby floor, I was crouched behind the front desk.

"May I help you?" Abe asked in a voice as smooth as cream.

"I'm looking for my sister. She came in here a few minutes ago to visit a sick friend."

"Was she carrying a rather large wooden case?"

"That's her. Could you tell me which room she's in?"

"Are you acquainted with the woman your sister is visiting?"

"Can't say that I am, but I can assure you that I've only the best intentions."

"I'm not questioning your intentions, son. It's just that we have rules. Why don't you take a seat and wait. I'm sure your sister will be along shortly."

"Wouldn't mind if I do. Must be near a hundred degrees out there."

"I hear it's going to get even hotter," Abe said.

The floor creaked from Seth's footsteps, then creaked again, closer that time, not moving away. Then the footsteps were to the right of the desk, and then coming around and stopping behind me. "What's this?" a female voice asked.

I remembered the voice, and it made me cringe.

"This, my good Mrs. Kingsley, is a telephone message I'm writing out for you. Read it, then get on back to your work."

I chanced a glance up and Mrs. Kingsley was reading from a piece of paper. She glanced down at me, then hurried away.

The lobby went quiet then, except for the rustle of papers. News-papers, I guessed, though turning too fast for thorough reading.

Minutes passed, and I was surprised by Seth's patience. I could only imagine what vile scheme he had in mind. To steal the Eclipse No. 3, to charm me out of my clam-cooking money. Or worse. It was hot as blazes under that desk, but I shivered anyway.

The whoosh of the front door opening promised hope for my aching knees. "Sure is a scorcher. There's hardly a soul on the streets," a male voice said.

"The heat has driven most folks indoors, including that fellow over there."

More footsteps. "Where'd you get that tattoo?" asked the voice I was then sure belonged to the constable.

"That'd be my business, now wouldn't it?" Seth answered.

"I think it is my business, Mr. Silver. And I'm placing you un-der arrest."

"You've got me confused with someone else. Name's Seth Martin."

"I'll be asking you to put your hands behind your back."

"You've got the wrong man, I tell you. Now unhand me."

There were sounds of a scuffle then, and Abe hurried to join in. I didn't know what I could do to help, but I wasn't about to just crouch there like a frightened child. I shot up, and my sudden movement must have distracted Seth's attention. "You?" he said, and in his moment of hesitation, he stopped fighting just long enough for the constable to snap the handcuffs about his wrists.

"Yes, me," I answered back.

There was no charm in the glare Seth shot at me then. Only harm. And his voice cut me to the quick. "Hasn't been a jail that could hold me yet. I'll find you. You can count on it, and then you're going to pay."

"Shut your trap," the constable said, shoving Seth toward the door. Before going out, he turned to me and asked that I leave my name and address. He'd need it for his report.

"I'll get you for this," Seth shouted from the front steps, and then he was gone. But his glare still stabbed at my eyes. His threats still roared in my ears. And my hands shook as I tried to grasp the pen Abe gave me.

Mrs. Kingsley was beside me then, offering a glass of water. "I watched it all from the hallway, and I don't know the whole story, but I'm thinking I misjudged you that day you came around looking for work. If you're still interested, you could start tomorrow."

The water calmed me, and when I'd emptied the glass, I took a deep breath and said, "Thank you for the water, ma'am, and thank you for the offer of work, but I've found work that suits me better elsewhere."

Mrs. Kingsley's smile faded into the grooves of her frown. "Fine," she huffed, then turned and walked away.

When she was out of earshot, Abe leaned close and whispered, "Two girls quit on her only yesterday."

I grasped the pen again and though my hands were still a bit shaky, I managed to write my name. I wasn't quite sure about the address, so I wrote two—the rural delivery route for back home in Nebraska and a note describing the location of the *Oh My*.

Back on the *Oh My*, with Isaac hanging on my every word, I relived the details of my afternoon. Telling helped calm my jitters, though it didn't take them completely away.

Work that Monday was a blessing for my hands, though it wasn't a blessing for my eyes. Seth lurked in every shadow. Every movement just beyond the edges of my sight. He was every man on the street whose face was turned away from me. Seth was in every night creak or groan of the *Oh My* as again and again I startled awake.

BANK ROBBERY SUSPECT ARRESTED

PRAIRIE DU CHIEN, WISCONSIN—Mr. Samuel Silver, also known as Seth Martin, was arrested yesterday in the lobby of the Dousmen House Hotel by Constable Carter. The arrest was made possible by the quick thinking and heroic actions of Miss Megan Barnett, a young woman from Prairie Hill, Nebraska, who is currently visiting our fair city. According to Constable Carter, Miss Barnett had seen Silver's wanted poster in Muscatine and identified him by the dancing girl tattooed to his forearm. In addition to being wanted for the thefts that landed him in the Fort Madison Jail from which he escaped, Silver is a suspect in last week's robbery of the Traders Bank in Moline.

Chapter 23

FOOLED

CONSTABLE CARTER CAME BY THE *OH MY* THAT MONDAY EVENING. HE pulled out a chair and made himself at home. "Not a bad little boat; how'd you come to own her?"

"Honestly," Isaac answered. He then explained about working in boat repair winters and spending summers on the river.

"You're living most every man's dream," the constable said when Isaac had finished.

"Was, until I hurt my leg. Since then we've had a pretty rough go of it."

The constable turned to me then. "I've had several reports about this Sam Silver. He's been thieving and conning his way up-river the last few weeks and nobody's been able to catch him till now. Tell me. How did you come to identify him?"

I told the constable my story, and he wrote notes in a pad as I talked. When his questions for me ended, I asked one of him. "What's the likelihood that Seth, I mean Sam Silver, will escape?"

"I heard those threats he made to you, but you needn't worry your pretty little head about it. I've got him locked up tight, and there's a federal marshal arriving by train tomorrow. He'll be escorting Silver back to Fort Madison."

I was about to ask exactly what time of day Seth and the marshal would be boarding the train, what time of day I could stop seeing Seth in every shadow, when Constable Carter turned again to Isaac and asked, "Did you happen to spend some time in Rock Island on your way upriver?"

"Nearly a week," Isaac answered.

"Did you take on a passenger there?"

There was something in the tone of this question that hinted at trouble. Isaac and I exchanged glances, and then Isaac said, "Is there some kind of trouble we should know about?"

"Could be."

"Well, we've done nothing wrong, I can assure you of that."

"Then you shouldn't have a problem answering my questions."

"I'd like to know what the trouble is before I answer any more questions."

The constable opened his folder, took out a paper, and slid it across the table. Isaac's brow furrowed as he read, and when he had finished, he slid the paper across the table to me. I read it twice and even then I had a hard time letting the words sink in. "But he healed your leg," I finally blurted. "He *must* be a real doctor."

"If you believe what's written here, then I guess he's not."

Constable Carter leaned forward. "Tell me what you know."

Confusion was hammering so loud inside my head I didn't hear the story Isaac told Constable Carter. To be mistaken about Seth was one thing; to be mistaken about Doc, or whoever he was, was quite another. He'd healed Isaac's leg. He'd sweated it out in the boiler room. He'd been a friend to all of us. He'd given me the gift of the Eclipse No. 3. *The Eclipse No. 3!* If what the paper had said was true, it hadn't been his to give.

When Isaac finished, Constable Carter closed his notebook and said, "I'm inclined to believe that you're innocent of any wrongdoing, but I'd like you to stay in town until I've checked out your story. Meantime, I'd be obliged if you turned over any property the imposter left behind."

I retrieved Doc's things—the medical bag, the medical books, the piscatorial finery, and suit of doctor-like clothes he'd worn into town the night we'd arrived in Prairie du Chien. I lay these things on the table before Constable Carter, then carried in the box of photographic supplies Doc had purchased in Dubuque. The Eclipse No. 3's case never felt so heavy as when I lifted it to the table, so heavy it might as well have been an anchor. When I finally let go of it, I felt as if I'd been set adrift.

Lastly, I handed over the photographs I'd taken. Constable Carter shuffled through them. "You take these?"

"Yes, sir."

He restacked the photographs then and handed them back to me. "I don't think the good doctor down in Rock Island will mind if you keep these."

"Thank you, sir. They mean a great deal to me."

When Constable Carter left, I collapsed into one of the chairs, my knees so weak I wasn't sure they'd ever hold me up again. I turned to Isaac then and said, "I can't believe we were all fooled."

"Hannah suspected something wasn't right, the way Doc always had his nose in those medical books, the stories of all the things he'd done. But I think she sensed that he was a good man, under it all."

"But he gave you medicines. What if he had given you the wrong ones? What if they had done more harm than good?"

"What if he hadn't? Some other doctor along the line might have amputated, and then where would I be today? I can't help but be grateful for that."

"But he stole the real doctor's things."

"If he were here to defend himself, I think he'd say he 'borrowed.' Remember, he told me we should return his things on our way downriver."

"Except for the Eclipse No. 3."

"Well, there is that."

The loss of the Eclipse No. 3 weighed heavy on me that next week. Instead of daydreaming over the cooker, my thoughts kept coming back to how foolish I'd been. Foolish to trust Seth, foolish to trust the imposter, foolish to think that I of all people would find a pearl. Foolish to think that I'd ever be anything but a mother's helper. Without the daydreams, the joy in the work was gone. Without the daydreams, I was working only to buy a ticket home.

When I stopped by the post office Wednesday of that next week, the postmaster had a letter waiting for me. From Mama. I tore into the envelope on my way out the door and read the rest standing in the middle of the sidewalk. I hadn't read far when I realized that Mama's letter was like clamming. The pearls of homey news that I'd longed for just weren't there. Her letter was scrawled with worry. She'd talked to Mrs. Humphrey, who'd talked to her brother-in-law, who had a third cousin who had once worked on a Mississippi River steamboat. "Says the river draws nothing but hooligans and thugs," Mama wrote. "I can't believe how foolish I was to say you could go, and I won't have a minute's peace until you're home where you belong. Hannah's a grown woman, and I can't tell her what to do, but I'm near heartbroken that she's exposing my grandson to a life like that. Don't you go anywhere unless you're with Hannah or Isaac. And don't you be talking to any strangers. Now, when you get home, things will be like they've always been, and you needn't worry about having idle time on your hands. Lila says you can start helping her right away. She's gotten behind on her mending and her garden's coming due, so she's going to need you to do the canning."

I'd piloted the *Oh My* and tended her boiler. I'd learned to swim and ride a bicycle. I'd taken passing good photographs. I'd cooked and cleaned enough mussel shells to supply the entire state of Nebraska with pearl buttons. I'd dreamed of one day opening my own photographic studio. Dreamed of spending my summers in my photographic studio on wheels, my very own automobile. Soon enough I'd be going home to a needle and a canning pot. I broke three times as many shells that afternoon as I'd broken in all my time working for Mr. Beauchamp.

I got so blue that I began thinking it would have been better if I hadn't turned Seth in. I'd at least have had the Eclipse No. 3. I knew it was wrong to think that way, but it's easy to slip into wayward thinking when you have nothing left to look forward to.

Isaac, on the other hand, was downright cheery. His wound had healed, and he'd given up his crutch in favor of a cane. He'd finished the fireplace mantel and had begun work on a parson's bench, and Hannah and Jon-Jacob would be returning soon. The only chink in Isaac's sky-high mood was the Pitman yoke. It had not arrived, though Isaac's boss in New Orleans had sent a telegram saying that he'd put it on a packet bound for St. Louis, with promises from the captain to see that it was transferred to another packet heading north.

I began stopping by the steamboat office on my way home from work those days that I'd heard a steamboat whistle a landing. I liked the steamboat office. No one there seemed to care one way or the other if I was wearing trousers, and the fellows hoisting the crates and barrels of this and that didn't smell all that fresh, either.

Chapter 24

JUDGMENT DAY

MARKING X'S ON THE CALENDAR HAD BEEN A MORNING RITUAL ON THE *Oh My*, beginning the day Hannah and Jon-Jacob boarded the train for St. Paul. "Twenty days left," Isaac would say. Or "Fifteen." Or "Eleven." My count was different than Isaac's. "Twenty-six. Twenty-two. Eighteen." Days I had left until *I'd* be going home. On the morning of July 31, I did more than count. I rolled that date around in my head, trying to scratch a nagging memory itch. And then it hit me. The Reverend Herman and his end-of-the-world prediction. I mentioned this to Isaac, and he had a good laugh. "Pick about any day, and there's somebody out there, somewhere, ranting and raving about it being the last."

I was somewhat assured, and the air wasn't unusually hot, the sky didn't show signs of a firestorm, so I pedaled off to work. I didn't forget about it, though. All that morning, working over the shells, I made my own accounting, just in case I found myself instantly raised up to the pearly gates. I wasn't sure what Saint Peter would think about my skipping church or if he'd think I'd loved the Eclipse No. 3 too much. I was even less sure about not writing the whole truth to Mama and Hannah in my letters, but was most unsure about the idea of judgment itself. Would Saint Peter take one look at me in my trousers and ruined shoes, reeking of mussel juice, and judge me unfit for heaven? Or would he take the time to get to know me first, review my entire report card, so to speak? I decided that he would take careful measure. He had the time, after all. And, unlike me and the wrong judgments I'd made that summer, Saint Peter had had lots of practice. So it was with a mostly clear conscience that I set off for the steamboat office after work—to learn that the Pitman yoke had still not arrived.

Water Street was especially busy that evening. Like the *Oh My,* the bicycle was at the bottom of the pecking order of vehicles, and I was forced to steer at the edges. At one point, I became so squeezed between a passing wagon and the wooden sidewalk that I was forced to apply the brakes, hop off, and wait until several wagons had passed. As I was standing there, I noticed a man. He was sitting on a bench, a newspaper held up in front of him. Next to the bench was a duffle and pinned to the duffle was a square of lettered cardboard. Letters that formed words. Words that fisted my gut.

HAVE YOU SEEN OR HEARD OF THE *OH MY*?

Had Seth escaped? Had he come back to make good on his threats to harm me? No, the man's hands were strong, sturdy, where Seth's had been fine boned. Seth's friend, then, come in Seth's place to take his revenge? Or was it something else entirely? A messenger, perhaps, sent by Hannah. Who else knew that the Oh My *was tied up in Prairie du Chien? Mama knew!* And I knew— that no matter how much my heart was racing, I couldn't just run away.

"Why do you want to know about the *Oh My?*" I called. The newspaper came down, revealing the man's face. The bicycle thudded to its side. Horace belonged in Plattsmouth, working in a door factory, not sitting on a bench on St. Feriole Island.

Horace jumped to his feet. "I can't believe my eyes—I can't believe that I've finally found you!"

Horace belonged in my memories of the moving train, not standing there on a solid, wooden sidewalk. I stepped back and asked, "You've been looking for me?"

"For weeks and weeks," he answered, erasing my backward step with a forward step of his own.

Horace belonged in my dreams, not there in flesh and blood, grinning. "Why? Why have you been looking for me?" I asked.

"I've got a good reason, you have to believe me," Horace answered as he reached into his vest pocket and pulled out what looked to be a fold of newspaper clippings.

I'd believed Seth, I'd believed Doc. I bent to upright the bicycle.

"Please don't go, at least not until you've read these clippings. They explain everything."

I was about to hoist my leg over the bicycle's bar when Horace began to read aloud from one of the clippings—an article about Isaac injuring his leg. I lay the bicycle back down, plucked the clipping from Horace's hand, read it for myself and asked, "Where did you get this?"

"I told you how I am about newspapers, how I can't resist reading them from front to back. I found that one lying on a bench in the Burlington station."

"And how was it that you just happened to be in the Burlington station? You said you were going to spend the summer building doors."

"I was, but the factory burned to the ground the very day I arrived. It's here, in the second clipping. Anyway, I figured it was a sign that I was supposed to do something more adventurous with my summer, so I hitched a ride in an empty freight car on the next day's Eastbound."

"With the intent of following me?"

"No, not at first. I figured I'd find work on a tow or a packet, something that would get me out on the river, but then I found this article about your brother-in-law getting hurt, and I got worried for you. I've been following your news ever since."

"My news?"

"You don't know, do you?

"Know what?"

"You've been making news all along the river. It's all here, in the clippings," he said.

"May I read the rest of the clippings?"

"Please do," Horace answered, handing them over to me.

I read the second article, about the burned factory, and got wide-eyed at the third—an article about Samuel Silver escaping from jail. And my eyes got even wider with the fourth—which implied that I was Seth's accomplice. "There's not an ounce of truth to this."

"Well of course there isn't any truth to it, and I told the Burlington constable as much. Told him you'd be about as likely to take up with a crook as he was likely to take up knitting."

I read my way through the fifth, sixth, seventh, and eighth, and had parked myself, woozy with astonishment, on the bench before I'd finished the ninth. "This one has nothing to do with me."

Horace grinned. "In a way it does. When your trail led me to Rock Island, I went down to that dock where your boat had been tied, foolishly thinking I'd find a clue to where you'd gone, and there, at the base of one of the pilings and just below the water line, lay a mussel. I'd learned something about clamming from fellows I'd met along the river, so I pried it open with my pocketknife, and lo and behold there was a pearl inside. The pearl buyer paid me eighty dollars. Enough to keep me following your news trail, with enough left over to pay my tuition come fall."

My thoughts raced back to Rock Island, to the mussel that had been blown back into the river by the thunderstorm. Could that have been the mussel that Horace found? It wasn't probable, but it was possible. Eighty dollars' worth of possible!

"What great luck," I said, hoping my voice wouldn't betray my twinge of envy.

"I owe my luck to you. If I hadn't been worrying and searching for you, that mussel would still have its jaws clamped over the pearl and doing whatever else mussels do."

"It was sweet of you to worry about me. I have made some mistakes this summer, and I've had some close calls, but here I am, still in one piece, so you worried needlessly."

"Oh, I stopped worrying four days ago, when I ran across the article about you being responsible for the arrest of that fellow who escaped from jail."

"That was in the papers, too?"

"Bottom of the stack."

"What did you do, read every newspaper between here and Burlington?

"Got to know the insides of a lot of railway stations and newspaper offices. Wasted my time in most of them, though— Davenport, Clinton, Dubuque, Galena. You must not have stopped at any of those towns, else I'm sure you'd have made news in those places too."

I couldn't help but smile, a little. A full grin would have said something I wasn't quite ready to say. "What did you expect would happen when you found me?"

"In the beginning, when nothing but trouble seemed to be coming your way, I suppose I thought I'd be your knight in shining armor, sweep in and rescue you."

"And once you realized I didn't need to be rescued, why did you continue searching for me?"

"I couldn't just quit. Finding you had become my treasure hunt, my quest, my one grand adventure."

"And now that you've found me?"

"Until now, finding you was everything. But now that you're sitting here beside me, I know what was driving me all along. You opened my eyes, Megan, back there on the train. And now that they're open, I just can't stop seeing things I would have missed before. Like the way the inside of a mussel shell looks white, but when you tip it this way and that in the light, there's a rainbow of color hiding there. The seeing itself isn't enough, though, and I'm guessing you already know that. For the seeing to count for something, it has to be shared. But not just with anyone. I tried pointing out some amazing sights to fellows I met along the way, and they looked at me as if I'd lost my marbles. So I guess that's what it comes down to. You're the one person who understands."

Any lingering doubt I had about Horace's intentions drained away. "I don't know what to say."

Horace smiled an impish smile and said, "Say you're glad to see me."

I looked at Horace, really looked at him, for the first time since he'd appeared from behind the newspaper. And what I saw took my breath away. The Horace of Plattsmouth was one and the same as the Horace on St. Feriole Island. The Horace of the train was one and the same with the Horace sitting next to me on the bench. He wasn't Seth. He wasn't Doc. He was Horace, genuine through and through, and he'd spent his summer searching for me!

I threw my arms around his neck, pecked a kiss on his cheek, and said, "I'm more than glad, I'm overjoyed. And I'm overjoyed that I didn't scare you off with all of my questions."

"I wasn't about to leave, not after having worked so hard to find you. Besides, you pelting me with questions is how we became acquainted in the first place. Remember?"

I think I blushed. "I remember, and in that way, I guess I haven't changed. But I think it's only fair to tell you that I'm not the same silly girl you met on the train. I wear these men's trousers day in and day out, and I tend a clam cooker and reek of mussel juice most of the time. My hands are chafed and calloused. But I feel no shame in these things, only pride."

"You should be proud. Now, instead of a delightful girl, you've grown into a delightful young woman, and I can't wait to hear how these changes came about, to hear the parts of your story that fit in-between the newspaper articles."

"That could take the rest of the summer."

"I have the rest of the summer."

Isaac was a little skeptical when I introduced him to Horace, but, like me, he warmed to him as soon as he'd read the newspaper clippings and heard Horace's story. And when Horace told Isaac about his studying to become an engineer and about his skill at fixing most all things mechanical, Isaac asked him if he'd trade a padded woodbin bed, free chow, and passage downriver for taking a look at the leak in the *Oh My*'s boiler pipes and for helping to install the Pitman yoke when and if it ever arrived.

"I was hoping you'd invite me, else I would have had to stow away," Horace replied to Isaac's offer.

"Kind of hard to stow away on a boat this size," Isaac said.

"I'd have lashed myself to the paddlewheel then."

Isaac slapped Horace's arm. "I understand, son. The Barnett sisters have that effect on us helpless fellows."

"Hush," I said to Isaac. "Horace and I are just friends."

"Close friends," Horace added.

Isaac and I wrote confession letters to Hannah before we turned in that night. It was time. I wrote about Seth, and I didn't leave anything out, not the stolen railway ticket, not his chilling threats. And then I wrote about Horace, and I didn't leave anything out there either, especially not the part where he thought I was the most delightful young woman he'd ever met. Isaac wrote about Doc and Constable Carter, who had stopped by several days earlier, saying that our stories had checked out and that we were free to leave Prairie du Chien whenever we liked.

PLAY MERITS RAVE REVIEWS

Not in That, I Won't, a hilarious three-act comedic play, opened Friday at St. Paul's Grand Opera House to rave reviews and sellout crowds. All acts were staged within a single set— the living quarters of a small and rickety riverboat, occupied by a young married couple, Hester and Isaiah Bradley, and their son, Joshua. As they travel upriver, a cast of strange and often bizarre characters drift in and out of the young family's lives. The playwright, H. Bradshaw, was on hand to assist Mr. Wallencott II in directing the play. H. Bradshaw, to the surprise of everyone in the theater company, turned out to be Hannah Bradshaw, a 22-year-old woman. Bradshaw's five-year-old son, Jon-Jacob, played the role of Joshua Bradley and nearly stole the show with his natural exuberance and charm. The leads, Miss Jacqueline Kepler and Mr. Thomas Greely, were both superb and gave performances that were quite convincing. The play runs through Sunday, August 9.

TOGETHER AGAIN

THAT NEXT WEEK HORACE STOPPED BY MR. BEAUCHAMP'S EVERY DAY AT lunch. These were leisurely lunches because, besides tinkering with the *Oh My*'s boiler and engine, Horace took over as errand boy. His first day out, he came by Mr. Beauchamp's with the news that the Pitman yoke had arrived, and he'd made arrangements for a dray to deliver it that very afternoon. I was thrilled, of course. Once the new Pitman yoke was in place, the *Oh My* could do what she was meant to do, steam free on the river again. At the same time, I puzzled over Horace's seeming good luck. He'd found the pearl I'd possibly overlooked. On his first day of visiting the steamboat office, he'd magically scared up the Pitman yoke. *Did one make his own luck, or did luck simply happen?*

* * *

Horace would be there on the *Oh My* at the end of my day. Our favorite place was the rooftop garden, the chickens clucking away in the background. I filled Horace in on the parts of the story he hadn't learned from the newspaper clippings, but no matter where I started, I always came around to talking about the Eclipse No. 3. "Remember on the train, when you asked me what my dream was and I didn't have an answer?" I said one evening. "Well, I know now. My dream is to become a photographer."

"With your gift, I've no doubt you'll be one of the best. And speaking of gifts, I've been wondering what you'd think of the idea of me giving you the gift of a new camera."

Horace's offer was tempting, as tempting as hot water and lavender soap after a day at the cooker, but I knew in my heart it wouldn't be the same. "For the camera to be truly mine, for it not to feel like I'm wearing someone else's clothes, I need to find a way to earn it on my own. Do you understand the difference?"

"How did you get to be so wise?"

"Practice," I answered.

Every day of my last week at Mr. Beauchamp's, he'd greet me with the same lament: "I'll never find another partner who can tend my cooker as good as you." On Friday, he went so far as to ask me if I had a friend who could take my place. I had to bite my tongue to keep from laughing. Between the long hours at the cooker and smelling to high heaven of mussel juice every day but Sunday, I'd not had a chance to make any friends, unless I counted the stray dogs who came sniffing around. I was about to tell Mr. Beauchamp that I was sorry, when I remembered the one person I'd met on St. Feriole Island who might indeed be interested.

I stopped by the Dousmen House Hotel on my way home that day and waltzed right into the lobby, trousers and all. It took Abe the time it takes to form a frown before he recognized me, but when he did, he greeted me with a hearty handshake. "You spy another criminal?" he asked.

"No, but there's a girl working here, as a laundry maid. She's about my height and wears her hair in one long braid. Might you know her name?"

"That'd be Mary Kingsley."

"Mrs. Kingsley's daughter?"

Abe nodded. "She's not in trouble with the law is she?"

"It's nothing like that. If I write a note, will you see that she receives it personally?"

"For you, missy, it will be my honor."

Abe didn't wait until the next day to give my note to Mary. He hand-delivered it to the Kingsley house on his way home from work that evening. And Mary didn't wait until the next day to see Mr. Beauchamp about the job. She'd gone to his home straightaway, though it was half-past nine. She was already building the fire under the cooker by the time I arrived at Mr. Beauchamp's that Saturday morning, and she was wearing trousers, which Mr. Beauchamp had told her were a must. She'd had to sneak the trousers out of her brother's drawer and out of the house. "Is it true, what Mr. Beauchamp said, about earning between four and six dollars a week?" she asked after Mr. Beauchamp had pushed off into the channel.

"It's true."

"Hallelujah," Mary said. "No more laundry."

"Tending the cooker is hard work, too, and smelly."

"You don't know what they pay at the hotel, do you?"

"No, your mother ran me off before I got that far."

"Well, they pay laundry maids three cents an hour."

"Oh my."

Mary was a fast learner, and with the two of us working side by side and chatting nonstop, we finished off the mountain of mussels by early afternoon. Mary was seventeen and engaged to a young man who was farming a little piece of land east of Prairie du Chien. He wouldn't get married, though, until he'd paid off his debt. Mary was hoping to hurry that along with the money she'd earn working for Mr. Beauchamp. "If we don't get an early cold snap, icing up the river, Mr. Beauchamp ought to be able to keep right on clamming through November," she said, then started counting on her fingers.

While she counted, I looked out over the back channel and tried to imagine the river in winter. It didn't seem possible that a body of water as wide and swift moving as the Mississippi River could freeze. *Would it happen overnight, or, like the stock tank in the barnyard back home, would water give up its heat to the colder air in tendrils of rising fog, and would it be possible to capture this rising in the lens of a camera?*

Mary finished her finger figuring and then shouted, "I'll be married by Thanksgiving! This is my lucky day."

I was glad for Mary, and even a little proud that I'd played a role in making it her lucky day. I did, however, keep a keen eye on Mary as she felt for pearls in her share of the shells, for fear that it'd be just my luck if she found one. She didn't.

Hoping that some of Mary's and Horace's good luck might have rubbed off, I took extra care with my touch, especially on the fifth- . . . fourth- . . . third- . . . and second-to-last mussel. Then, in the last shell of my last day of tending Mr. Beauchamp's clam cooker, the last shell of the thousands I'd cooked and pried open, the last shell of all last shells, I found . . . nothing but smelly, slimy, pearl-less mussel meat.

Mr. Beauchamp paddled in soon after, and the shell buyer arrived soon after that, and soon after that Mr. Beauchamp counted out my share of that week's earning and laid each bill in my open hand. One, two, three . . . and I'd done it, earned my ticket home. Four, five, six . . . with three dollars to spare. Seven, eight—a bonus for finding Mary. And nine was for, "Ah, heck. Nine's because I'm going to miss you."

Horace, Isaac, and I spent our Sunday up to our elbows in grease. Elbow grease, for scrubbing the *Oh My*'s windows and floors. Lard, for two peach homecoming pies. And axle grease, for all the engine's moving parts.

And then came Monday morning. Hannah, writing that she was so anxious to get back home, had purchased tickets on a night train out of St. Paul. They'd be arriving at the station at nine o'clock. As Horace and I prepared to leave for the station, Isaac was wishing out loud that he could come with us to meet the train. "How about the wheelbarrow?" I suggested. And that's what we did, Horace volunteering to push.

Isaac abandoned the wheelbarrow as soon as we arrived. And when the locomotive whistled its approach, he handed his cane to me. And when the train came to a stop, and Jon-Jacob flew down the coach car steps, Isaac held his arms wide. Hannah, following close behind, let Mama's carpetbag fall to the platform and soon the three were intertwined in homecoming. I thought of Mama. I took up Horace's hand and squeezed it tight.

The party we had around a roaring bonfire we built on the shore that evening was perfect. By turns, we danced to the lively music Isaac played on his harmonica, we laughed, we whooped, we pitched and skipped rocks into the river. We made so much happy noise, in fact, that we drew out the man whose shoreline we'd been tied to for nearly a month. The man Isaac and I had often seen, though never spoken to directly.

"Having a party, are you?" he asked when he'd made his way down to the shore.

"I'm sorry if we disturbed you," Hannah said.

"Me and my wife, we used to build bonfires like this one, before she passed on. Got to remembering those days and just had to come on down. Hope that's okay."

"Glad to have you," Isaac said, standing and offering his hand. "Name's Isaac Bradshaw."

"Zeke Stowe," he said, shaking Isaac's hand.

"I've been wanting to thank you, Mr. Stowe, for letting us tie up here," Isaac said. "We'll be leaving in the morning, so you'll be getting your river view back real soon."

"So your secret work is done, then?"

"Secret work?"

"That fellow who was with you the day you came. That government fellow, he said you were here doing some secret work for President Cleveland. Undercover work, and that's why you'd be dressing and acting like ordinary river folk. Said I shouldn't disturb you, shouldn't mention your comings and goings to anybody. Hope you won't turn me in for coming down just this once. The wife, you know."

"We won't say a word, will we?" Isaac said looking around our circle. We all shook our heads.

We steamed away from Prairie du Chien at daybreak the next morning. Like leaving Mama behind at the Prairie Hill station, I held St. Feriole Island with my eyes until I could no longer see her.

Traveling with the current was very different than fighting against it, the river itself doing much of the work of the boiler, engine, and paddlewheel. There were still the snags and traffic to worry about, but we all took turns at piloting, including Isaac, and that spread the worry out, making the time spent on the river almost leisurely. When not piloting or tending the boiler, I spent a great deal of my time at the rail, framing scenes in an imaginary camera, or straining to see who was manning the cookers in the clamming camps that dotted the shores on either side of the river.

Afternoons were spent exploring towns and cities we'd hurried past on our way upriver—Galena, Navoo, Clinton. The size of these towns, I decided, could be measured by the number of smokestacks puffing dirty clouds into the sky. Smokestacks that reminded me of enormous candles, with the flame just snuffed out. Most of these cities had at least one photographic studio, and most of the studios had photographs displayed in their windows, and most of the subjects of these photographs were people—stiff-backed, unsmiling, wooden-looking people. All the cities had newspaper stands, at which Horace left some of his pearl money.

Evenings, Horace and I cut wood. Horace and I fished, and I actually landed a good-size carp without falling overboard. Horace, Jon-Jacob, and I took long walks along the shore to give Hannah and Isaac time alone. After nightfall, Horace and I read his newspapers by lamplight, though he said some of the fun had gone out of it since I'd stopped making news. I didn't read for fun. I read for Seth. Read the headlines for his escape. Read the middle pages for his escape. Read the back pages for his escape, read as carefully as I'd searched mussel shells for pearls.

I didn't find Seth, thankfully, but, in a week-old Rock Island paper, I found Doc. I was astonished at first, and then glad. When passing the mouth of the back channel leading to Dr. Miller's summer home, I sounded the *Oh My*'s whistle three times.

MISSING MAN RETURNS

ROCK ISLAND, ILLINOIS— James Downy, a former patient and handyman of Dr. Matthew Miller, who was earlier accused in a theft at Miller's summer home, returned of his own accord Wednesday last. Mr. Downy claims to have no memory of the time he was away, and, as most of the stolen property has been returned by a party who gave Downy passage upriver, Dr. Miller has asked that the charges against Downy be dropped. "He wouldn't hurt a soul," Dr. Miller said when asked why he'd taken Downy back into his employ. One mystery remains. Among the returned items was a photographic camera, which Dr. Miller claims to have never seen before. The camera is being put to good use, however. Downy has set up a photographic studio in Dr. Miller's downtown office and is taking photos of patients, free of charge, while they wait for their appointments.

Chapter 26

LAST DAYS

WE SPENT TWO NIGHTS IN MUSCATINE, TIED NEAR THE CAMP OF THE clamming teachers and wolf-whistling parrot, whose manners were not much improved. I walked the same path I'd walked before, carrying an envelope as I'd done before. The difference was that Horace walked beside me, and the envelope did not contain a letter to Mama. We made three stops that morning. The first was at the post office, where I was relieved to find that Samuel Silver's poster had been taken down and that there was not a new one saying that he'd escaped from jail again. Our second stop was at the Boepple Button Factory Store, where I spent a quarter buying five cards of pearl buttons. One each for Mama, Lila, and Hester, and two for myself. Our last stop was at Mr. Greenwald's photography shop. I wasn't in the window.

Mr. Greenwald must have seen me standing there, staring at nothing. He met us at the door of the shop. "Come on in," he said with a gentlemanly sweep of an arm.

"You're as lovely as I remember," he said to me, then turned to Horace. "And I'm glad to see that you found her."

"It took me a while, and a good dose of luck, but I finally caught up with her in Prairie du Chien."

"What happened to my photograph?" I asked.

"Probably could have sold you to Mr. Harris, the undertaker. After I put you in the window, he'd come by every afternoon on his stroll and then tell anyone who might be passing on the sidewalk that he'd made your acquaintance, and what a delightful young woman you were."

I remember the too-tight grip on my arm. "If not the undertaker, who then?"

"Could have been any number of smitten young fellows, coming in here and begging me to tell them your name and where you lived."

I think my cheeks might have pinked because Mr. Greenwald turned to Horace then and said, "I think it's time we told her."

"It was me," Horace said. "I left my pocket watch with Mr. Greenwald in exchange for him taking your photograph out of the window and holding it for me until I could return with the money to pay for it."

"Your watch? You shouldn't have."

"I figured, if I didn't find you, at least I'd have your photograph as a reminder to always keep my eyes open."

Mr. Greenwald brought out my photograph then, and it was *my* eyes that opened wide. At first I thought he'd made a mistake, that I was looking at another girl's face, or that Mr. Greenwald knew some kind of photographic trick that hadn't been included in the Eclipse No. 3 instruction booklet. A trick that made plain girls appear beautiful.

"It's not like looking in a mirror, is it?" Mr. Greenwald said. "In the right hands, a camera captures more than flesh and bone. It captures the subject's spirit."

I pulled my little stack of photographs from the envelope and shuffled until I came to *Egret in Calm*. "Like this?" I asked, handing it over to Mr. Greenwald.

He studied it for a moment. "Who took this?"

"I did, with an Eclipse No. 3."

"May I see the others?"

I handed over the stack, and Mr. Greenwald spent a good bit of time studying each one, and when he'd finished he lay his hand on my shoulder. "If you can do this amazing work with an Eclipse, I can only imagine the quality of images you'd capture if you had professional photographic equipment."

If pride were a color, mine was as iridescent as the inside surface of a mussel shell.

Horace and I spent three hours at Mr. Greenwald's shop, and I came away with several pages of notes I'd taken on lenses and developing techniques and exposures in varying types of light. And a list of professional-grade photographic equipment I'd need if I were serious about becoming a photographer. Serious didn't describe it. I was on fire with the possibilities. Horace came away with the photograph of me, wrapped in brown paper, and his pocket watch.

That evening, near nightfall, Hannah and I bathed at the mouth of the creek where I'd had my first swimming lesson.

I'd just finished working a lavender lather into my hair when Hannah said, "We'd love to have you join us again next summer, if you're interested. It won't be fraught with the problems we've had this year, I promise."

I dunked my head in the water, to rinse the suds away and to settle once and for all a debate I'd been having with myself. While underwater, I thought it through one more time and it came down to this—the *Oh My* was Hannah's home, not mine; the river was Hannah's life, not mine. We were sisters, but we dreamed different dreams, and, just before my lungs burst, I surfaced with my answer. "Just the thought of leaving here, leaving the river, the *Oh My*, and all of you, nearly breaks my heart, but it would break my heart even more if I never pursued my dream of becoming a photographer. For that to happen, I think I need to find year-round work back home, be it mother's helper or laundress or ditch digger. But, once I've started making a living as a photographer and find that I have a little extra money burning a hole in my pocket, I'd love to join you again, for a week or two, anyway."

"You have an open invitation on the *Oh My* any time of year, be it on the river in summers or down in New Orleans the rest of the year. Whenever and for however long you'd like to stay. Perhaps you and Horace—"

Hannah didn't get a chance to finish her sentence because I splashed her, and then dunked her, and then splashed her again.

We arrived in Burlington with only one day to spare. After tying up the *Oh My* at nearly the same spot where I'd first laid eyes on her, we all went ashore. At McDougal's General Merchandise store, Isaac sat with Jon-Jacob while a clerk fitted him for new shoes. Horace went off to look at men's trousers, and Hannah steered me toward the women's ready-made clothing department. "I need a new suit to replace the moth-eaten one, and I'd like your opinion. If you were me, which would you choose?"

"That one," I said, pointing to the one whose dusty rose color reminded me of sunsets on the river.

"This one it is, then. And of course I'll need a new hat to go along with it." We giggled over the more lavish ones, which had so many lacy ruffles and velvet flowers attached to the top, they looked like flowerpots. I pointed out a simple one, tan in color, with a brim that was wider in the front than in the back and set off by a band of black ribbon. Hannah plunked it on my head, stood back, and then said, "I'll take it." And then we went off to join the fellows in the shoe department. The clerk must have gotten a look at my shoes, because he came up to me right away and asked what style I wished to try.

I was about to tell him that I wasn't there to buy when Hannah leaned into my ear and whispered, "Go ahead, just for the fun."

So I sat down and removed my shabby shoes. My cheeks probably matched the dusty rose of Hannah's new suit when one of my toes poked through the hole in my stockings. Thankfully, the clerk pretended not to notice. "What size?" he asked.

I had no idea. Every pair of shoes I'd ever owned were in the size of whichever sister was handing them down to me. Hannah suggested a seven, and the clerk brought out three pairs: the Sunbeam, the Wonder, and the Charmer. All buttoned up the side and were made with the softest kid leather. All pleased my feet, but none so much as the Wonder, which had a squared-off toe instead of a pointed one. "The price?" I asked, actually considering spending some of my clam-cooker money.

"Two dollars and fifty cents," the clerk answered.

Two dollars and fifty cents would buy me an MC Rapid Rectilinear Lens. I'd go barefoot first. "I'll have to think about it," I said to the clerk, who wasn't as pleased as my feet had been.

Upon leaving McDougal's, we divided. Horace and I went off to the train station while the others went in search of a grocery. The station, though still grand, seemed smaller somehow, the hands on the station clock less taunting. I asked the fare to Prairie Hill and then counted out $11.20 of my clam-cooker money, which would have taken me a third of the way toward owning a Carlton Reversible Back, 5" x 8" camera. My forty-cent telegram to Mama would have bought a dozen sheets of Kloro Aristotype Printing Paper. "Will arrive 3 PM Saturday. Megan." What more was there to say?

Chapter 27

GOODBYES

WE SPENT OUR LAST NIGHT TIED TO THE SAME ISLAND AS THE FIRST, though I didn't cut wood and I didn't eat cold biscuits. Hannah's farewell supper surprise was a Swedish dish she had been introduced to while in St. Paul. It was called Sjömansbiff, or Sailors' Stew, and was made with strips of flank steak, onions, potatoes, and exotic spices my tongue was thrilled to make the acquaintance of.

After supper, Isaac invited me to walk with him along the shore. He used his cane, though leaned on it only lightly. "It's been quite a summer, hasn't it?"

"Quite a summer, indeed."

"We can't thank you enough, Megan. Without you coming up with the idea of the leeches and maggots, I might have lost my leg.

Without you, Hannah would have missed out on seeing her play performed. Without you—"

"It's me that should be thanking *you*," I interrupted. "If you hadn't agreed to let me spend the summer with you, I might never have had a chance to try my hand at photography. That's what I'm going to do with my life. I don't know how yet, or when, but I'm determined."

"Then it'll happen," Isaac said.

Hannah had a second farewell surprise waiting for me when Isaac and I returned from our walk. There on my bunk lay the dusty rose suit, the banded hat, the Wonder shoes, and a full set of not yellowed, not stained, not holey, not mussel-juice scented, underthings. "What's this?" I asked.

"It's our gift to you. You are too stubborn to accept money for all the help you gave us this summer, and I know how you feel about wanting to earn a new camera for yourself, but I'm your sister and stubbornness is one of the many things we have in common. No arguments. When you get on that train tomorrow, you'll not be wearing someone else's wedding suit. These lovely things make a statement about who you are—a competent, self-assured, and exceedingly beautiful young woman."

It's hard to argue when your heart is bursting with joy.

* * *

Horace had become Jon-Jacob's pal on our trip down the river. Horace's skipped rocks often kissed the water seven or eight times before disappearing. Horace knew the best places to look for garter snakes, and his cannonballs sprayed tree-high plumes. So it wasn't surprising that it was Horace Jon-Jacob came to that night. "Why do you and Auntie Megan have to leave?"

"We have important things we need to do, things we can't do here on the *Oh My*."

"What kind of things?"

"Well, Megan needs time to plan out how she's going to make her dream of becoming a top-notch photographer come true for her, and I need to finish my schooling so I can design and build a top-notch automobile."

"You mean like me having to wait until I'm all grown-up to become a top-notch actor?"

"Exactly, my little man," Horace answered.

But it was me Jon-Jacob came to the next morning. He climbed into my lap, pearl-like tears running down his cheeks. "I love you, Auntie Megan," he sniffled, "and I don't want you to go."

I kissed his damp cheeks and then said, "Remember how your papa missed you terribly when you were up in St. Paul, and remember how excited and happy he was when you came back to him? I think your grandma and grandpa Barnett might be missing me like that."

"But you're all grown up."

"I don't think they see me that way, at least not quite yet."

"Maybe they need eyeglasses," Jon-Jacob said in his most serious voice.

"How did you get to be so wise?" I asked, then tickled his tummy, and his seriousness gave way to giggles and smiles.

I was smiling, too, when I covered myself in dusty rose. The trousers had been just the thing for river travel and clam cooking. My old skirts and shirtwaists were just the thing for a mother's helper. The dusty rose was just the thing for a young woman to wear into her future.

Horace didn't smile, though, when I stepped out of the pantry. It's hard to smile when your pinky fingers are stuck in the corners of your wolf-whistling mouth.

Then it was time to say my goodbyes to the *Oh My*. I smoothed a wrinkle in the fish quilt. I tidied an already tidy shelf in the pantry. I checked the boiler gauges, twice. I plucked a weed from the rooftop garden, and I bid the hens goodbye and good laying. I bent over the navigation charts, noting the location of a wing dam just south of Burlington. Then, in a final salute, I pulled the cord of the steam whistle. WHORAROARAROAR. WHORAROARAROAR. And then, Mama's musty-smelling cartpetbag in one hand and the picnic basket in the other, I crossed the *Oh My*'s boarding plank for the last time. I didn't look back. Didn't need to. She was, indeed, a swan.

The Westbound, steam rolling out of her locomotive stack as if from the nostrils of an impatient bull, was already boarding passengers when our little group arrived on the platform of the Burlington station. "I'm so proud to be your sister," Hannah said, gathering me into one last hug.

"I'm going to miss you so much," I said, then finally let go of the tears that had been building behind my eyes. A river of them.

If not for Horace tugging me away, the train might have pulled out of the station without us. When I'd reached the coach car's top step, I turned and choked back my tears enough to shout, "We Barnett girls are really something, aren't we?"

"We are indeed!" Hannah shouted back.

Chapter 28

HOMECOMING

PERHAPS IT WAS THE SPEED WITH WHICH TOWNS AND TREES AND fields and cows flew by the train window, or perhaps it was that I had Horace by my side, but the next twenty hours felt like no more than four or five. We talked. We laughed. We napped on each other's shoulders. We played the seeing game. We read each other stories from the newspapers passengers had left behind. We got off at the longer stops and stretched our legs. We stood on the little platform at the rear of our car, stuck out our tongues, and tasted the wind. We stuffed ourselves from the overflowing lunch basket. We made promises to each other, though never so fervently as we did while the Westbound waited at the Lincoln station. We'd write, at least once a week, to share amazing sights and to encourage each other not to falter in our resolves. Horace would take the train to Prairie Hill on his Christmas break, visit me on the farm, meet my parents.

As the Westbound began to pull away, Horace lifted my chin. It was the kind of kiss I'd seen Isaac give to Hannah. I didn't close my eyes the way Hannah did though, and neither did Horace. Seeing had brought us together in the first place.

I don't remember much of the flat, empty space between Lincoln and Prairie Hill. Empty of Horace. Empty of Hannah, Isaac, Jon-Jacob, and the *Oh My*. Empty of the river and the rolling green bluffs. Empty of all that had been my summer—except for the $5.43's worth of hope I carried in the pocket of my dusty rose suit.

Denton. Highland. The whistle of the last country crossing before Prairie Hill. The chug-a-choos slowing. The Methodist cemetery. The backside of Sloan's Eatery. The platform of the Prairie Hill station. Mama and Joey, there on the platform—wearing the same clothes and standing in almost the same spot where I had left them, as if they'd been frozen in time.

The conductor collected Mama's musty-smelling carpetbag and the lunch basket from the baggage bin, then moved aside and said, "After you, miss." My Wonder shoes made quick, graceful work of the coach car steps. Mama kept looking past me, like she was waiting for the old me to show herself. But Joey, dear sweet Joey, winked a brotherly wink and then said, "Hey, sis, you're looking real spiffy."

Mama woke up then and rushed to me. I pulled her into the

first hug we'd ever shared. And Mama hugged me back. It felt good there, good to be home. Mama unwrapped me, took a step back, and then said, "Well, let me have a look at you." She looked me up and down, then reached out and ran a hand over the sleeve of my dusty rose. "Lovely," she said, "but what have you done with Lila's wedding suit?"

"It's in the bag along with a gift I've brought for you."

I bent to open the carpetbag and to retrieve the photograph I'd taken of Hannah, Isaac, and Jon-Jacob. I handed it over to Mama.

Mama raised her free hand to her mouth and tears sprang to her eyes.

While Mama was studying the photograph, Joey pulled a letter out of his trouser pocket. "We stopped by the post office this morning, and this came for you."

I took the letter from him and read the postmark—Fort Madison, Iowa. A thunderbolt shocked through my body. The letter was from Seth, I had no doubt about that. And he knew my address, knew where I lived. The old tremble returned to my hands as I stuffed the letter deep into the belly of the carpetbag.

"Aren't you going to read it?" Joey asked. "I had to sign for it, so it must be important."

"Later," I answered, then returned my attention to Mama.

She'd pressed the photograph over her heart.

* * *

On the wagon ride home, Mama and Joey kept up a steady report of what I'd missed while away. The Fourth of July picnic at the church, the tornado that had just missed the farm, the circus that had come to town, the funeral of a neighbor who had fallen when trying to repair a leak in the roof of his barn.

I only half listened, what with wondering how far downriver the *Oh My* had floated Hannah, Isaac, and Jon-Jacob in the time since we'd said our goodbyes in Burlington. What with wondering if Horace had settled into his dormitory room, and if he had yet freed my photograph from its protective paper wrapper. What with Seth's letter burning a hole in my homecoming.

Mama had planned a welcome-home party for me that evening. Everyone was there—Hester and Lila and their families, including the babies that bulged their bellies. Jake and Alice, Papa, James, and Joey. And Hannah's family, too, in the photograph Mama set on the mantel. "Look, but don't touch," she warned everyone. Even Papa.

Mama had made rice pudding for dessert. "I made it special for you," she said, a full ladle hovering over my plate.

Maggot memories churned my stomach. "That was sweet of you, but I'm so full of your chicken and dumplings I can't eat another bite. Truly, I can't."

"I'll save some then, for tomorrow."

I nodded. Tomorrow would have to take care of itself.

After we'd cleared away the supper dishes, I presented Mama, Hester, and Lila each with a card of pearl buttons. They presented me with their thanks and a chorus of oohs and ahs. There would be time to share my dream with them in the days to come, but there was one conversation I didn't want to postpone. I excused myself and went in search of Papa then. I found him out on the front porch, lighting his pipe. "Good to have you home," he said, shaking the flame off his match.

"It's good to be home, sir," I replied, then added, "I met a young man, his name is Horace Blount, he's seventeen and a student at the University of Nebraska. We've become quite good friends this summer, and have promised one another that we will keep in touch through letters. Hannah and Isaac think quite highly of him, as I'm sure will you when he comes here for a visit on his Christmas break."

Papa took a long draw on his pipe, let the smoke out slow, then asked, "What's he studying?"

"Engineering, sir."

Papa lifted a brow. "Admirable profession," he said, then drew another puff on his pipe.

That was answer enough for me.

That left just one other thing that couldn't be postponed—the Fort Madison letter. Bad news was like souring milk. It didn't get sweeter with time. I waited until everyone had gone home or turned in for the night, then sat at the edge of my bed. My hands were quaking so badly by the time I shook the contents of the envelope out, a narrow slip of paper fluttered to the floor. Leaning close to the kerosene lamp, I unfolded the letter and read so fast that when I reached the end, I had to go back and read it again, word for word, to make sure I'd read it right and to give myself time for the words to sink in. The letter wasn't from Seth; it was about Seth. He'd been transferred to the Iowa State Penitentiary. This was made necessary because of Seth's previous escapes, and because of the seriousness of his recent crimes, which included, among other things, robbing a bank in Moline and breaking into an elderly woman's home in Guttenberg, threatening her with a knife, and then stealing her money. "The good citizens of towns and cities bordering the upper Mississippi River are forever grateful for your quick thinking and bravery in the capture of Mr. Silver. Enclosed you will find a bank draft, made out in your name and for the full amount of the reward." The letter was signed Mr. Patrick Jones, Lee County Iowa, District Attorney.

Mama would ask me the next morning what that sound was that she'd heard coming from my room the previous night. She might have heard my thump as I slipped off the edge of the bed in my haste to retrieve the slip of paper from the floor. I'd righted myself, leaned my back against the bedpost, and read, *Pay to the order of Megan Barnett, the sum of Two Hundred Dollars.*

She might have heard the WHORAROARAROAR of my heart. She might have heard the door to my photography studio swing open with such force that it tore itself away from the hinges, and the engine on my automobile chug as I bumped along river roads and mountain roads, deserts and seashores, wherever my eye to the lens would take me. Yes. That's what Mama heard.

GALWAY COUNTY LIBRARIES